Soul of A Warrior

by

Faith V. Smith

Viking, Go Home

Semper Fi Magick

Cover Art by Debbie Taylor

The Wild Rose Press
PO Box 708
Adams Basin, NY 14410-0706
Visit us at www.thewildrosepress.com

Publishing History
First Fantasy Rose Edition, 2015
Print ISBN 978-1-5092-0002-3
Digital ISBN 978-1-5092-0120-4

Published in the United States of America

"If ye do not quit thrashing around, woman, I will not be responsible for taking you."

"Taking me where?"

"Thor's hammer, I meant as a man takes a woman."

Raven didn't have to see the blush on her face—she could feel it. The man must think her bonkers to not know what he meant. She could only blame it on an overprotected childhood and a desire to start and keep her career moving.

Mortified beyond belief, she tried again to escape. Her hand brushed something hard against her thigh. Her gaze caught and then fell into dark silver spheres staring back at her.

Before she could open her mouth, his lips locked on hers, the covers disappeared, and a firm but gentle hand found and then slid under her gown. Her breath caught, held, and then released into his warm mouth as his fingers climbed higher. His tongue swirled deeper and taunted her until she reciprocated.

Wulf's foray to find and tease all her trigger points made Raven burn with need. Her hips rose off the mattress when his hand found her breast.

His mouth released hers. "Easy, Raven. There is so much more I want to do to you. I do not want to hurry and your need is reaching out to me too fast and too hot."

"Too bad, Viking. You started this, so don't complain to me if you can't keep up."

Viking, Go Home

by

Faith V. Smith

Dedication

To my darling Rick, who could have been a Viking, and to my talented daughter, Amanda.

Also to Gini Rifkin who always loves my work, Mark Zickefoose, whose talent for fixing my computers keeps me going, and to all who were pulling for this book to be published. Also to Eloise Cornell who always waits breathlessly for my next book. To my brother Rod, thanks for believing in me. To Sarah Hansen, my wonderfully talented editor, thank you from the bottom of my heart! As always to God be the glory!

Chapter One

House of Thorrason
Norseland 1016

Wulfgar Thorrason unlaced his braies and prepared to mount the auburn-haired beauty in his bed. It had been several sennights since he rode away to settle a dispute at the edge of his property. His kinsmen had received his return with jubilation and a feast. After feeding the gnawing hunger in his belly with roasted meat, vegetables, and nuts, he'd quenched his thirst with an abundance of mead.

Weary from his travels and drunk as the next man, he'd fallen facedown on his bed to awaken with a bedmate. Now his morning shaft begged to find haven in the woman's softness.

As he prepared to do just that, the room darkened and all around him the world went still. The woman on the bed froze with her arms out in a beckoning manner, the lustful smile on her red lips now etched in a frozen parody.

Wulf, as he was known to his friends (what few he claimed), laced his pants and lunged for his double-edged sword on a trunk at the foot of the bed. Before he could follow through on his instinct to kill whatever evil spirit dared enter his longhouse, a shimmer of color appeared and then formed into a tall, buxom silver-haired blonde.

Her features were refined, her brows an arch of color above emerald green eyes that glared at him. Sunrise-pink lips sat below a dainty nose and her chin tilted up at a slant.

"Who are you?" His voice rasped through the

room. A tone that usually scattered friend and foe alike did not even make the woman flinch.

"I am Catriona, princess of the Norseland faeries. You are to remain silent. Your lustful ways have created havoc amongst the mortal realm and faery kingdom. I have irate fathers threatening to punish all of your kind because of you. The last bit of my patience was used up when you seduced my niece and left her crying."

"But, I—"

"Silence! I have passed sentence on you, and I am here to see it is carried out. From this moment on, until you learn that lust is not love, you will be banned from your homeland."

"What? Surely you jest. Why should I believe a wench who says she is a faery princess?"

"Believe me or not, Viking, you will learn what true love is, or die far from home."

Again, he tried to reach his sword, but with a wave of the woman's hand, his arm dropped to his side. His body went rigid, and the world caved in around him. One moment, he stood inside his bedchamber—the next he was spinning rapidly through space.

"Heed my words well, Thorasson, or you shall never see your homeland again."

****

Raven Harrison grabbed her digital camera and slung its cord around her neck, stuck her cell phone in the back pocket of her jeans, and grabbed a backpack filled with her wallet and a thermos of soup before snagging her car keys. She had about an hour of daylight left to get pictures of one of the ancient gravesites near her home.

Nana Bella had raved about the mausoleum with etchings of medieval times engraved on the outside. It was her goal to get a few quick shots, load them on her laptop, and then enlarge them. She wanted to study the pictures in hope they would reawaken her creative side. Caroline, her editor, would kill her if she missed her latest deadline.

The cemetery came into sight, and she pulled in close to the fenced off area. The seat belt strap sang as it was released and gravitated back to its anchor. A second later Raven stood in the brisk almost-winter Michigan weather, looking up at the six-foot obstruction to her goal. Nana had omitted telling her about the fence. The backpack hit the grass, and she grabbed the wire and began to climb.

Her sneakers made a soft *thud* when she landed on the other side. A well-used path headed to the right and she followed it. After conversing a curve, she stopped in amazement. Row after row of ancient headstones greeted her.

Where to start was the question.

Never one to procrastinate, Raven unslung her camera and began snapping shots as fast as she could. Inside the cemetery the trees stood close together. Their almost-bare branches lent an eerie air to an already spooky atmosphere.

Gathering her courage she moved between the markers and got her bearings. She scanned the landscape looking for the mausoleum she'd come to find. Straight ahead, atop a hill, the bronze-colored stone glistened in the rapidly failing sunlight. The wind picked up and sent a shiver across her spine.

Too bad she had to leave her backpack outside the fence. Soup would do a lot to take the sudden chill from her bones. She tugged the sleeves of her sweater farther down over her wrists in an effort to cover some of the exposed skin on the top of her hands.

The camera's cost had set her back royally. She didn't want to drop it.

Black clouds formed on the horizon and began to push rapidly to where she stood. If she wasn't mistaken there was also a bit of mist in the air.

She took the rise at a fast trot. Better to get the

pictures before the weather turned worse.

Once in position, Raven clicked away, trying to cover as many angles as possible of the building. She eased around the side of the granite, and the wind began to howl with a gale force shriek.

Saints alive. The weatherman hadn't mentioned anything about stormy weather. Small branches, separated from the tall oak trees, twirled in a mad dervish. She ducked one flying object but a second one gave her a glancing and painful blow on the side of her head. Before Raven could stow the camera back around her neck and get her hands up to cover her face and head, another limb, bigger this time, spiraled right at her.

Stars exploded inside her closed eyelids before her knees gave way, and she hit the ground, a second before everything went black.

****

Wulf squinted his eyes against the driving rain. He raised his forearm and deflected debris from the storm. Wherever Catriona had sent him, he knew it was not home.

Nay, this place with its memories of the dead waxed much warmer than his native land. Still he was grateful for the braies covering his lower limbs and the infernal organ that led to his troubles.

"Ouch."

The faint cry caused him to start for a moment. He'd thought he was alone.

He cursed the wind and rain obscuring his vision, and suddenly the wind died. He wasted no time on wondering why but instead focused his gaze on a mound of color near a building. Tree twigs crackled and broke under his bare feet as he strode forward.

The mound stirred and then gained its footing. In its place, a woman stood. A quite damp and beautiful woman.

He cursed the lust begging his manhood to stir.

If he didn't need to marry and sire an heir, someday, he would almost wish to be impotent. Now with the prospect he might never see Thor House again, he needed to bridle any emotion below his waist.

Still, 'twould be harder than he thought as he got closer. The wet and busty siren finally glanced his way, and lips bare of any artifice opened in a delightful oval. Strong white teeth greeted him. A good sign if he were looking for a bride—which he was not. Strands of hair rained water down onto the front of her already drenched shirt. The material was not something he had ever seen before: bulky but caressing at the same time over her ample breasts.

Some type of man's garment, again material he had not seen, covered her shapely thighs and legs pulling his attention to the center of her womanhood.

"Hey, I don't know who you are but it's rude to stare like that."

Wulf's gaze reluctantly returned to her face. Eyes, blue and icy like the fjord in his village, glared at him.

"Forgive me, I have never seen a woman dressed the way you are."

"Are you putting me on?" She grasped, twisted, and wrung out her hair.

"I am not sure what you mean, but I speak the truth. Wulfgar Thorrason does not lie."

"Oh please...where did you come up with a name like that?" Again she wrung out water.

Wulf did not have a notion of what to say. Never before had a woman ridiculed him or doubted his word. The wenches and jarls' daughters all hung on his every sentence with sly looks and grasping hands—hoping to woo him into their beds, or in some cases wedlock.

" 'Tis a name given to me by my father." His tone grew harsh thinking of Magnus, his father, who was also the jarl of their village until his death. What he would say to his only son if he were still alive? His father believed in power, honor, and love. The first one Wulf had in abundance, but he was sadly lacking in honor and love. Oftentimes, he had taken what women offered him without caring if he left them with a part of himself. Only by the grace of the Christian God his father had revered that he did not have an abundance of children running free.

"You're kidding, aren't you?" The woman flung her hair behind her head and looked him fully in the eyes, piercing him with her icy blue gaze.

"Nay, if you mean I am lying to you. 'Tis true, I was given that name at birth."

"I suppose you also developed your mode of dressing from your father?" The quizzical look in her eyes held curiosity.

" 'Tis the way the men in my homeland dress. Of course, normally, I have on a tunic and vest, as well as my boots."

"So, where is home?"

"Norseland." Wulf moved a bit closer to the woman, maybe the wench would be able to tell him where and what year it was.

Blue eyes stared and then blinked. "Oh, you mean Norway?"

"I'm not sure what it is called now. I just know when I left home, my land was called Norseland."

"Look, I don't know where you came from or if you hit your head during the storm, but I've gotta go." Raven stepped back from the giant man standing in front of her. Ever since she'd come to after the tree branch beaned her, she wondered if she had a concussion. This sexy and almost-naked man was crazy. Just her luck. Running around in the cold air with barely a stitch on and spouting nonsense about homeland. She wished the behemoth would go away. Her head was splitting, and she wanted to get home.

"Please, I need to ask you something."

"Make it quick." No way could she stand to look at him much longer. Her pulse skittered with more than the effects of the freak storm. His eyes were so light, they shone silver. His hair rippled, a dark cloud of coal. A strong jaw and full lips—extremely kissable lips—only turned him into the equivalent of a hot hunk of sensual granite. Which meant he belonged to someone else. No way would he be unattached.

"I need to know what year it is." The man's voice rasped along her spine. She wondered if he would sound that way after making love. His tone also carried a hint of confusion.

"Well"—Raven looked down at her wristwatch—"when I left home a couple of hours ago, it was October 16, 2010."

The man's previously tanned face turned the shade of one of the gray headstones. His eyes widened, and he took several deep breaths. The force of the air entering and leaving his body showcased his broad and almost smooth chest.

" 'Tis impossible. Surely the princess wouldn't send me to the future? Not even a faery could have that much magic, could they?"

She watched the disbelief in his dilated pupils, heard it in his words, but the man was crazy. There was no such thing as time travel. Sure, she saw it in movies, read about it in romances, but get real. Still...as inspiration, he was more than enough to get her author juices flowing—not to mention her feminine side.

"Look, I think you probably need to see a doctor. Maybe you have a concussion or something." Raven drew a bit closer to Wulf or whatever his name was. "I can call someone who can help you."

He looked down at her from his impressive over six-foot-four advantage.

"I do not need a healer if that is what you mean.

I be not sure what a concussion is, but I do know I be in a time not my own."

Raven resisted the urge to hum the tune to one of the old sci-fi television series.

"Okay, well then, maybe I can give you a lift? You know back to where you live?"

As she watched, he seemed to grow in height. "I told you, I am from Norseland, and I was born in the year 976."

"Look, buddy, I'm sorry, but I think you're off your rocker. Besides, if you *were* from that time period, how come you can speak and understand English?"

"I do not know, maybe Catriona made it so I could understand. Look, I told you, woman, I am a Viking."

"And I have two words for you, *Viking*: go home."

Chapter Two

Before Wulf could gather his words to reply, a sound like metal hitting rock bounced off the building near them.

The woman jerked and squeaked, then grabbed his arm.

"Someone's shooting," she hissed. "We have to get out of here."

For one so much smaller than he, her grasp was strong. He allowed her to pull him down the hill, as more sounds echoed all around them.

"Hurry up, do you want to get killed?"

She towed him along until they reached some type of wire fencing. The woman grabbed the wire and began to climb rapidly to the top.

"Get a move on, will you? Those are bullets not popcorn coming our way."

Another round of sound and the dirt in front of his feet bucked up.

"God help us!" Her voice conveyed the urgency he was beginning to feel, and Wulf followed the woman's lead and began to climb, all the time wondering what else could go wrong.

Once over the side, she moved to a large metal object. He jumped back with alarm when she opened it up and climbed in.

She growled at him. "What are you waiting on, an engraved invitation? We have to go."

Wulf copied her prior movements and tried to fold his body into the small area.

"Shut the door, Viking."

He looked and then found what looked like a lever. He grasped it and then pulled it forward—

enclosing himself inside with, as much as it hurt to admit, his rescuer.

"Whew, looks like we made it." Raven's heartbeat began to slow somewhat, but her hands still trembled. "I have no earthly idea why someone was shooting at us, but I'm definitely calling the police."

Raven looked over at her passenger. Wulf's face still had not regained his previously tanned color. The man's hands gripped his thighs in such a way, if he wasn't built like he was, he'd leave bruises. For pity's sake, she wasn't driving all that fast. You'd think the man had never been in a car before.

Well he said he was born in 976. She shushed the tiny voice in her head. Time travel was a myth. He probably just didn't like female drivers... Still—

"Hey, you okay?"

"What is this thing?" His words were uttered through clenched teeth.

"What?" The man was more loony than she'd originally thought or a good actor. *Or maybe he's telling the truth.*

"This thing we are riding in."

"It's a car. Haven't you ever seen one before?"

"We do not travel this way in my time."

Raven gritted her teeth. "Look, you have to understand, what you're telling me about being from the past is totally crazy to me."

"As it is to me. I wish to return home, but I cannot." The Viking's voice held anger as well as regret.

"Okay, so let's say you're for real. Maybe I can help."

"I thank you, but Princess—"

"Whoa, princess? That's the second time you mentioned this princess. I think we need to talk. I'm going to hit a drive-through and pick up some food, and then we'll go to my place. I need to call the police about what happened, but after we eat, you can tell me your story."

"You would open your home to me?"

"Well, if what you're telling me is true, you don't know any one else in this century." Raven would weigh the pros and cons of having the seductive and hot bod in her house at a later time. For now, the man could use some help one way or the other.

"I do not even know your name."

A quick glance reiterated she needed to keep her eyes on the road. His silver eyes glowed with frustration and probably homesickness. Poor thing. She'd bet whatever caused him, if it was true, to be sent to the future had not been his fault. Poor baby.

"I'm Raven. Raven Harrison."

"Your father named you after a bird?

"Actually, my mother did. She used to do a lot of bird watching."

Apparently Wulf's curiosity was satisfied for the time being. He remained quiet as she rolled through a fast-food restaurant and ordered hamburgers, fries, and shakes.

Not long after that, she pulled into the circular drive of her home. Being an author had been a second job at first, but now with the revenue from her books, she'd put down a down payment on her first real home away from her childhood home.

After putting the car in park and turning off the ignition, she opened the door and got out. Raven walked around to the passenger side and opened the door for Wulf, who held the bags with their food. She retrieved the cardboard holder with the shakes.

"You about ready to eat?"

His puzzled stare went from her to the bags and then back again. "You eat parchment?"

Raven's laughter brought a slight smile to his lips.

"No, silly, the food is inside the bags." Unable to resist, she touched him lightly on the arm and couldn't help but enjoy the feel of taut muscle under her fingertips.

The man was built like a brick house.

She stepped back as Wulf finally managed to unwedge his body from the car. He stood silent while she closed the car door, and she motioned for him to follow her up the walkway.

One minute later they stood inside the entryway. After bolting the door, she started toward the kitchen.

"Let's eat."

When she turned after taking the bags from him and putting the food on the old farm-style table, she almost stepped on his bare feet.

Funny, Raven had failed to notice he didn't wear any type of footwear. She gave his scrumptious body a once-over and noticed the gold bands he wore on each massive forearm.

"What are those for?"

Wulf glanced down and then his gaze speared hers. "They are bands with my family crest."

"I see...a hammer for Thor?"

"Yea, but for Thorrason not the god of thunder." The slight grin he gave her revealed even and extremely white teeth.

"Come on, sit down. I'm starved." Raven yanked out a chair and promptly sat. Her hopefully short-term house guest did the same. She took a burger out of the bag, dumped it and a large order of fries onto a paper plate, and slid it across the table.

Not sure if Wulf knew what a straw was or how to use it, she prepped his shake and pushed it within hand's reach.

His eyes followed her as she took a bite of burger and crunched on a fry. He did the same. When she took a sip of her chocolate shake, he mimicked her move again, like he really had no clue as to how to eat junk food.

"This is good; I like it."

Raven hid a grin when he picked up a napkin

and dotted the catsup off his lips.

"I'm glad. When we finish eating, I need to call about the shooting at the cemetery, but after that I really want to talk to you about where you came from. Now tell me about the pendant you wear. Is it a family heirloom?"

****

Suddenly the tantalizing taste of meat tasted like ashes to Wulf. What if she still didn't believe him? And if she did, what then? Catriona's words he needed to learn love in order to return home made no sense to him. He'd cared for all the women he'd taken to bed. And there had been many. Raven would think him a womanizer. Why it should matter to Wulf, he did not know, but it did.

"Earth to Wulf. Did you hear me?"

"Yes, I am sorry. Of course, we shall talk about my home. My mother gave me the pendant when I became a jarl."

After gathering and tossing the remains of their meal, he followed Raven into a room she called a den. She motioned for him to sit. If he were not so beholden to her for a place to lay his head tonight, or if he were not dazzled by the now dry waves of blonde hair drifting over her breasts and the soft blue of her eyes, he would order her to stop treating him like a hunting dog to be commanded.

Once he did as she asked, he shrugged his shoulders. "You may ask your questions." He prayed his rescuer would believe him. Until he could figure out how to get home, he could not afford to make her think him more crazy than she already did. Thor's hammer, he certainly did not want to leave—just yet. Something about Raven called to him. He wasn't sure in what way, but it was more than lust that caught his interest.

The smile Raven shot his way bordered on irritated. Who did he think he was? Oh yeah, right, a Viking.

"Thank you, I believe I'll start with, what did you do to make someone mad enough to banish you from your home?"

"I uh...I was..." Wulf's words trailed off.

Yep, he was a bit perturbed. Good. He'd had her in a tizzy ever since they met. It was his turn now.

"You what?"

"I was accused of rutting too much."

Raven bit her lip until she tasted the salty tang of blood. Oh my Lord, the man got banished because he couldn't keep his pants up.

Well...maybe it wasn't all his fault. The women were probably all over him. He was more than a bit cute, he was hunk city with all the chocolate in the world thrown in for good measure.

"I see. So did you?"

"Did I what?"

The blaze of color turning his cheeks a deeper bronze was actually endearing, but she wasn't ready to let him off the hot seat. And she still needed to find out if his story was true.

"Have sex with all those women?"

This time Wulf's face turned a rich crimson.

"Ye should not be talking that way. Ye are a woman."

His statement threw her for a moment and then she laughed.

"Look. Viking warrior or whatever, this is 2010. Women not only talk that way but they actually participate."

Shock lanced through his eyes, turning them almost black.

"Do you participate that way?"

Heat scalded her cheeks. "That is none of your business, Mr. Thorrason."

" 'Tis Jarl Thorrason. And you asked me, so I'm asking you."

Raven cleared her throat. "Well, I think this conversation is finished. Why don't I show you where the bathroom is..." Her words trailed off at his look of confusion.

"It's a place you can take a bath and take care of any *personal needs.*"

Her guest stood up when she did, and followed when she moved out of the kitchen and to the bathroom. He flinched but did not say a word when she turned on the light. He moved closer when she pulled back the sliding door to the walk-in shower and turned a knob.

"How did you do that?"

"You mean make the water come on?"

"Yea, I do not think you would be part of witchcraft, but how?"

The man was either an expert in reenactment skills, or as she truly began to believe, a visitor from the past.

"Water is channeled through underground pipes. There is a heater that warms the water when you turn one knob and then there is also a knob that makes the water run cold."

"Do you think I could try it?"

"Of course. Just let me check this and I'll leave..." Raven's words disappeared in a throat suddenly gone dry. Wulf, the split second she'd turned to test the water temp, stripped off his pants. His bottom half was just as impressive as his top portion.

In fact, the male portion of him, even unaroused, was way more imposing than she could have imagined.

She brought her gaze back to his face, and cringed at the smirk on his sensual lips.

"So you see, sometimes, I was the hunted instead of the hunter."

"So, you're telling me you just allowed yourself to be led to the slaughter...or should that be bedroom?"

"I may have allowed myself to be led to the

bedchamber, but I assure you once there 'twas I who did the leading."

Raven would have—should have—knocked the sensual smirk off his lips, but instead decided to do the prudent thing and retreat.

Moments later, she pulled a flannel gown from her clothes bureau and prepared for bed. She couldn't get the scene in the bathroom out of her mind. Sure, his chest had looked just fine in the *kitchen*. Well, actually, a bit more than fine. Muscular and probably warm if she'd dared to touch his bronze skin, but combined with a full frontal sans braies, Wulf oozed testosterone until her knees almost buckled. Something she would definitely have to guard against if he stayed.

Stayed? That would be pure lunacy on her part. The man was a walking advertisement for sex. She certainly didn't need him in her life, and she positively did not want him anywhere near her bed.

Raven snorted out loud. Maybe if she said it enough, she might believe it. But that was the least of her worries. Somewhere between the cemetery and the shower, she'd found herself warming to him, not just the physical perfection of Wulf, but his smile, his accent, and his old-world charm.

Just her luck to pick up a stray that could be endearing, obstinate, and would make a great sex toy.

Whoa. Don't go there, girlfriend.

The man was just staying the night, and then she'd find him a nice hotel until she decided if he should be committed. Or, if he spoke the truth, she'd help him find his way back home.

Once in bed, she flicked off the bedside lamp and settled under the covers. Ten minutes later, she still lay awake. The Viking's movements in the adjacent guest room filtered in through every nook and cranny. Why didn't he go to sleep? She was more than ready for a good night's sleep after today. She frowned. Crackers, what with listening to Wulf and doing a more than adequate fill of looking at his drool-worthy body, she'd forgotten to call the police about the shooting at the cemetery. First thing in the morning, she'd fix that mistake.

Wulf's muffled exclamations on finding and exploring new objects finally ended, and Raven took advantage of the quiet and closed her eyes.

A creaking noise woke her sometime later. She punched her pillow and tried to go back to sleep. Wulf undoubtedly suffered from insomnia. Raven turned on her back and stared straight into the eyes of a masked man.

Chapter Three

"Who are—" Her question was cut off by the pillow smothering her face. She struggled to pull it off but the man caught her hands with one of his. Her nose closed up, and her throat did the same as the oxygen she needed to breathe was denied.

Raven's lids closed and behind them, dark spots formed. She tried to lift a leg to knee her assailant in the groin, but couldn't. So not fair. She didn't want to die in bed taken out by her own pillow.

Her frantic gasps for air slowed and so did her movements. She fought her way through the Lord's Prayer when a crash against the bedroom wall coincided with the pillow being tossed aside. Before she could gather the strength or the breath to fight off a new attacker, two hands grasped her arms and tugged her upward.

"Woman, be you all right?" Wulf's tone smacked of apprehension and drizzled fear.

"I'm fine, Wulf. Thanks to you. If you hadn't..."

For the first time since he'd rescued her, she looked around. "Where is—"

"Do not worry about him, he will be no trouble for a while."

"That's good to know." She clasped one of his arms with her hand.

"Thank you for saving me."

"You do not need to thank me. You opened your home to me. I thank you."

Raven had one brief moment to stare into Wulf's eyes before he brought his lips down on hers.

His kiss practically scalded her with its steam. His hands should be declared lethal, except the feelings his touch invoked deep inside her were anything but deadly. She felt alive, treasured, and yet fearful at the same time. His tongue teased and coaxed hers to play, before he removed his mouth all too quickly. His arms slid around her body, bringing them so tightly together she feared she would lose her breath once again.

"I do not like this time. Men should not attack women. 'Twould not be tolerated in my homeland."

The more she heard the truth in his tone, the more she tended to believe he might be from another time. As much as she would like to ask him more questions, there was an unconscious assailant on her bedroom floor, and she needed to call the police.

"Wulf, I need to get up and call the police." Raven eased from his embrace and swung her legs over the side of the bed. When her feet touched the floor, she staggered. A large arm encircled her waist, and she leaned against the Viking as she moved to the kitchen where she'd left her backpack. She unearthed her cell phone and punched in 9-1-1.

****

Raven slumped down on the couch in her den and rested her head against the back. The police had come and gone, taking with them her intruder and her sanity.

Officer Hamilton looked like she'd lost her mind when she told him about the incident at the cemetery. Even though Wulf had backed her up, Hamilton had acted like she was the little woman who'd allowed her imagination to get the best of her. All she'd gotten from him was they would "check it out." The other officer, a Detective Giles, seemed concerned, so maybe he would do something besides mouth platitudes.

Bully for them, maybe someone would take a potshot at the officers and then they would believe her.

And, just maybe, the break-in had nothing to do

with the earlier incident. She sure hoped so. Her deadline was imminent in her mind. If she didn't get a move on it, Caroline, her editor, would be calling.

Now she had an overgrown Viking with her for an indefinite length of time. She could take him to a hotel, but after tonight's episode, she rather liked having a man in the house.

Raven's body bounced slightly when Wulf sat down beside her.

" 'Twould be best if you tried to get some sleep." His gruff tone sounded compassionate, but no way could she go back in her room for what was left of the night.

Violated did not touch the way she felt. She'd been so proud of her new home. And now it felt tainted.

"I don't think I can sleep. Maybe I'll curl up here and just rest."

"If you be afraid, you could sleep in the room you gave to me. I'll stand guard so no one else gets inside."

His words comforted as nothing else could. She'd been on her own for so long, it would truly be a gift to have someone else take over—even for one night.

"That is so sweet of you. I don't know what to say."

"Just say yes, Raven. Sleep will put you in a stronger mind. Or at least 'tis what my mother used to say."

She forced her eyes to stay open; the events of the day were catching up to her, but she wanted to talk to Wulf.

"Is your mother still alive?"

"Nay, she passed to the other side after my father passed to Valhalla."

"I'm sorry. I lost my parents also." She leaned back against the arm Wulf slid across her upper back.

"Who has been looking out for you?"

Instead of jumping on him for assuming she couldn't look out for herself, she caught his hand and squeezed it.

"Thank you for caring, but women in my time are able to look after themselves."

"How?" His disbelief seemed real.

"Well, I write books and make money that way. Some women work in factories, some as nurses, and so on and so on. There are a lot of opportunities. Women even serve in the military."

"What is this military?"

"It's like Army, Navy, Marines, Air Force." Raven twirled a piece of hair between her fingers and scrunched up her face. "Warriors. They are warriors who protect our country."

"Women do this?"

"Yes, you have a problem with that?" Prepared to smack him if he went all macho, she waited for his answer.

"No, I am highly respectful of lady warriors. The Valkyries of Valhalla choose the warriors they feel are truly heroic."

"Oh, okay, just wanted to make sure you weren't a chauvinist pig."

Wulf's look of outrage caused giggles to erupt from Raven.

"I don't mean a real pig, it's a figure of speech."

"Good, I would not be wanting to be called a pig."

Raven laughed again and then with an almost tender look in his eyes, Wulf caressed her face.

"You need to sleep."

A yawn caught her unaware. "I guess I should, but I'm..."

"Sleep. I'll watch."

"Thank you, Wulf. I don't know why, I just met you, but I trust you."

"Go to sleep, woman." His gruff words were the last thing Raven heard before she succumbed to his order.

Wulf watched the woman he now held in his arms. He liked how she felt nestled next to him. Her breasts, as they rose and fell in slumber, teased his skin even through her sleeping garment.

Faint shadows rested below her lower lashes. He wondered if she was as fearless as she acted. His thumb touched her brow and traveled a path down her cheekbone to rest against her lower lip. He bit back a groan as he smoothed the slight pout adorning it.

His honor, previously hidden, reared its head. Raven had been through enough today. He should put her to bed and then leave her. And he would in a moment. For now, Wulf wanted to revel in the knowledge that this woman did not fawn over him, or play games. She said what she meant, and if he wasn't mistaken, Raven wanted him as much as he wanted her. Yet, he wondered if what he felt was just lust, or could it be the emotion Catriona called love?

Chapter Four

Raven awoke and tried to move her legs. The weight pinning them down did not budge. With her eyes still closed she wiggled a bit to her left and then right. Surely she couldn't have wrapped the covers so tightly around her body they wouldn't come undone.

A grunt in her left ear startled her, and then a large arm draped itself across her chest. Her eyes flew open, and she turned her head to look at the sleeping man lying next to her.

Mother, Mary, and Joseph. How did she end up in bed with Wulf?

She tried to slow her rapidly accelerating breaths so she could think. Finally, the night's events came back to her. Wulf's promise to protect her while she slept had been kept, but she didn't remember going to bed.

Oh Lord, did she still have her gown on?

Raven slipped one hand under the cover tucked up to her neck, and breathed a sigh of relief when she felt flannel. Oh, thank God! Of course if she had any sense, she would be bemoaning the fact the handsome Viking could sleep next to her and not try something.

Bad girl! Bad girl! Just be thankful. She could end up pregnant, since she really doubted the birth control they used in Wulf's time would be effective, and with no date life, she wasn't on anything either. Not that she needed to be on something. And although her fans might think she knew a lot about what went on in the bedroom, Raven still maintained her virgin status.

Okay, time to try getting up again. Putting action to her thoughts, she wiggled to get her legs our from under the massive tree trunks Wulf called legs.

"If ye do not quit thrashing around, woman, I will not be responsible for taking you."

"Taking me where?"

"Thor's hammer, I meant as a man takes a woman."

Raven didn't have to see the blush on her face—she could feel it. The man must think her bonkers to not know what he meant. She could only blame it on an overprotected childhood and a desire to start and keep her career moving.

Mortified beyond belief, she tried again to escape. Her hand brushed something hard against her thigh. Her gaze caught and then fell into dark silver spheres staring back at her.

Before she could open her mouth, his lips locked on hers, the covers disappeared, and a firm but gentle hand found and then slid under her gown. Her breath caught, held, and then released into his warm mouth as his fingers climbed higher. His tongue swirled deeper and taunted her until she reciprocated.

Wulf's foray to find and tease all her trigger points made Raven burn with need. Her hips rose off the mattress when his hand found her breast.

His mouth released hers. "Easy, Raven. There is so much more I want to do to you. I do not want to hurry and your need is reaching out to me too fast and too hot."

"Too bad, Viking. You started this, so don't complain to me if you can't keep up."

His snort almost brought a smile to her lips, but his hand found and then caressed her womanhood. A whimper escaped to be caught in mid-air by Wulf as he tasted her lips again.

Raven pushed against his hand and a spiral of

need built and then rose higher and higher. Just as she was ready to fall off the precipice of desire, the doorbell rang.

Wulf jumped and withdrew his hand, followed by the warmth of his body.

Shoot, she'd forgotten he didn't know what a doorbell was. Wait, back up the book. When had she truly started believing he was a time traveler?

The bell rang again before Raven could answer her own question.

"It's okay, someone's at the door. I'll be back in a minute." She tried to put him at ease, but he still looked a bit shell-shocked.

After leaving the bed, she smoothed her gown down her body, grabbed a robe, and answered the door.

"Are you Mrs. Harrison?"

"Actually, it's Ms."

"Don't matter, I have a special delivery for you. Sign here."

The boy grabbed his electronic clipboard back after she scribbled her name and took off down the sidewalk.

Raven closed the door against the early morning chill, moved to the kitchen, and sat down. She slid a finger under the large manila envelope, shook it, and watched as a single sheet of paper fell slipped out.

You have something I want. Meet me at the cemetery tomorrow night at dusk. Bring your camera. My associate failed to do what he was told last night, but I won't fail. If you do not meet me, then the next time I go after someone, it will be your boyfriend.

Her fingers trembled as she worried the edges of the paper. First the gunshots, then the attack on her, and now this. She should go to the police, but they probably wouldn't be any help. They seemed more interested in getting the heck back to the station last night and not her problem.

Still, she should at least let them know about

the note. Yeah, sure, then the entire PD would be spouting the local author's imagination was in overdrive. If they only knew what she wrote, then maybe they'd be more eager to help.

She balled the note up in her hand and tossed it in the trashcan near the counter. No, she'd handle this herself. She just wished she knew this person was and why they wanted her camera.

Only one way to find out.

Raven backtracked to the bedroom and went to the dresser to get her digital. Thank God the camera survived the trials of the afternoon. Wulf lay on his side with his elbow cradling his head.

"Is there anything wrong?"

She inhaled and then exhaled before replying, all the time plugging her camera into her laptop.

"No, everything's fine. I uh, just have some work to do."

The pictures loaded on the screen, and Raven enlarged and then studied each one. The first group was from a book signing earlier in the month, the second batch from the cemetery.

There was nothing to see in the shots she took leading up to the mausoleum, but one picture jumped at her. Grainy in contrast, but she could make out a man standing over another man lying on the ground. What looked like a gun pointed down toward the body.

Oh my gosh. This was it. It had to be. But she had no idea who the guy was. Maybe if she enlarged the picture more?

No, she still couldn't get a good look at his face nor could she see the other man's face.

What should she do? Now that she actually had evidence of a crime, if she went to the police, the man could make good on his threat to harm Wulf.

Her heart stalled and then started again. No. No way would she place him in danger. Beside the fact, he would probably be great in bed, yeah like she didn't already know that fact, she was beginning to care for the Viking.

"Raven?"

She pulled her mind back to the here and now and not what if.

"Yeah."

"Are you sure nothing is wrong?"

She forced a smile on her lips and then turned toward Wulf. "I'm positive."

"Good, now come back to bed."

As much as she wanted to, as much as her body would love to be seduced by his, she couldn't. Not until she had a concrete plan. She couldn't just go to the cemetery, hand over the camera, and hope the man wouldn't finish the job of killing her.

"No, I need to—"

"Raven, did I do something wrong?"

How could she tell him he'd done everything right? So right, she was afraid to go back to bed with him. To have him make delicious love to her and then be killed. Leaving her to grieve over something that was barely started.

"No, Wulf. You were great. I just don't think it's a good idea for us to be together that way."

Wulf tossed the sheet back and stood up. What had changed? Raven had wanted him earlier, been eager with the desire he shared. Something must have happened between the time she answered the door and she played with the little metal box with a humming noise.

"I don't understand." She eased out from under the hand he placed on her shoulder.

"There's nothing to understand. You are from another time. Anything between us would never work out. It's best to understand that now and not complicate things."

Wulf wasn't sure if what he felt was love, but his heart ached from the pain of what felt like a jagged sword thrust within its depths. For the first time in his life, since he came into his manhood, he cared, deeply cared, for someone.

How or why did not matter. It would not ease the band of iron pressing against his upper chest. What should he do? Leave? He didn't know if Catriona would even hear him if he called. Would she believe he now knew the difference between love and exercising his lust?

Before he could decide to try to talk to Raven once more, the little box she kept by the bed began to blast out noise.

Raven picked it up and placed it against her ear. He wasn't sure what she heard but at least the infernal racket stopped.

"No, I'll be there. Yes, I'm sure. I just forgot." She turned toward him, and her lips pulled up into a grimace before she spoke again.

"Give me an hour, there's something I have to do first."

Chapter Five

Wulf stood like a frustrated child while Raven poked and prodded the pants she'd told him to put on. The tough material rubbed his legs, but the under-clothing she said he had to wear felt soft against his deflated manhood. Not even stripping off in front of her in the small cubicle they were in caused even a spark of desire to shoot through him.

He felt like a piece of meat to be cooked and it did not sit well.

"Okay, now put this on and we'll get you some shoes."

"I do not see the need for all of this."

"Of course you don't, but I told you I have to go to a book signing. I can't just leave you at home."

"I be not a child, Raven. I can stay by myself."

The look she gave him as she smoothed out the short-sleeved apparel did not convey agreement at all.

"Please, just bear with me. It won't take more than a couple of hours and then we'll grab something to eat."

The thought of something to quiet the rumblings in his belly kept him quiet.

Earlier, once Raven stopped talking on the little box, she'd whirled like a devil. Dashing to and fro and then the water came on in the bathing room. No time to break their morning fast, and by the way the sun looked when they arrived at the shop, noon had long come and gone.

He kept silent and followed her into a larger room and then to a place where shoes sat all over. Peering closer, he examined shoes he'd never seen before. Before he knew it, a man rushed over and began to measure Wulf's bare feet.

"Tsk, tsk. The man has feet the size of a horse. I'm not sure if I have anything to fit."

Again he kept silent and remained still. The urge to tap the little man who insulted him was strong, but Raven would probably think him a barbarian as well as a child.

After having his feet crammed into several pairs of leather boots, Raven and the man settled on a pair of canvas-like shoes with laces.

Before he could say anything or knock the smug look off of the little toad's face, Raven tugged him away, flashed the hard little square called plastic she was so fond of, and then they were back in the car.

****

Raven dotted the *i* in her last name with more emphasis than necessary. She forced a smile as she handed the book back to her fan.

Her smile, however, disappeared as she scanned the large room for a glimpse of Wulf. The man had attracted every female in the room from infant to senior since they had arrived. She wanted to kill him, but truthfully, he'd done nothing to encourage the herds of drooling women. He almost looked desperate when she'd taken her seat to start the book signing and left him all alone.

The poor man, he could probably drop a fly with an axe or sword at fifty paces, but his face had turned almost green. Green was a color she could empathize with. Never in her life had she ever been jealous over a man, but when it came to Mr. Viking extraordinaire, she was ready to pour boiling oil over her fans.

Because his butt looked like a million bucks in the pair of skin-hugging jeans. And just because the pullover shirt brought into play all the rippling pecs and muscles in his upper body and arms, that was no reason to want to kidnap Wulf and escape back to her house with him before having her way for hours with Mr. Hot-and-Sexy.

No, no reason at all, except she wanted him so badly she could taste him, not to mention, she could feel her body's responses to him with peaked nipples and a subtle but definite wetness between her thighs.

Finally! She spotted Wulf at the back of the milling crowd. He glanced her way at almost the same time she saw him. The expression on his face looked a bit frantic. As he began to make his way toward the front of the room, he was stopped time and time again. Pieces of paper, even lipstick-stained tissues were thrust at him.

Raven started to rise from her seat but another fan stuck her book on the table.

"Here you go, my dear."

Raven tamped down her irritation. "How would you like this made out?"

"Just put it to Mixxy. And you know, my dear, I wouldn't worry about your young man."

Raven jerked her gaze upward. The elderly woman's blue eyes twinkled.

"He's not—"

"Honey, take it from someone who's seen a lot of this world, and buried three loving husbands. That man has eyes only for you."

"How can you be sure?"

"Well, I've been waiting for almost thirty minutes to get this far in line, and I've watched him as the women mobbed him. All the time, they were flirting, he was looking at you."

Raven's mouth fell open. "Oh...I didn't know."

"You do now, so sign my book and get the heck out of here. Take him home, bed him, and be grateful he's a one-woman man.

She autographed two more copies of her latest book before Wulf finally made it to the table. His group of followers only a step or two behind.

Should she stake her claim or not? As she made up her mind, one brazen hussy patted his butt.

Oh, hell no!

Raven slid one hand into the front of Wulf's jeans and tugged him forward before she stood up. She casually removed her hand, ran it down the side of his thigh, and then inched it around to his fanny.

"Hi hon, you about ready to go home?"

Bless Wulf's heart, he didn't even look shocked.

"Aye, I can't wait to get out of here with you."

Since he was behaving so well and saying all the right things, she lightly caressed his buttocks. Her reward, a singeing stare from his sizzling silver eyes.

"And if you don't be stopping what you are doing, we might have to finish our talk from this morning."

Raven knew her face was red—it burned—but the looks the women gave her were full of envy, and for a woman who always felt lacking when it came to the male population, she couldn't help but preen just a bit.

"Anything you say, darling."

Never in all the history of her book signings had she broken down her exhibits, and packed up promotional material so quickly. Of course, it helped there were no books left over for her to take home.

Lillian, her agent, and Maxine, her publicist, barely had time to say goodbye before Wulf almost pulled her out the door.

"What's the matter, Wulf, didn't you enjoy all the attention?"

"No, I did not. The women of your time are brazen. Only the trollops and bed wenches in my time behave that way in public."

"Well, you didn't seem to mind *that* much." She couldn't resist a jab at his expense. The man caused her concentration to go on strike during the signing.

It was a miracle she hadn't signed his name

instead of her own.

"Fie, woman, no man wants to be poked and prodded and to be looked over like a side of beef."

"Hmm…is that what you did with the women you bedded?"

His face changed expressions, going from outrage to confusion, and then a blank stare, so fast she would have missed it if she hadn't been looking.

"Methinks you are right. Could be the reason Catriona thought I needed a lesson."

Wulf caught Raven's arm as they moved to her car. He walked her around to the driver's side and then waited for her to unlock the door before opening it for her. Well, in a lot of ways, the man was a gentleman, and maybe this faery princess was off the mark a bit.

Once they were both seated and buckled up, she asked the question screaming in her mind.

"So, have you learned your lesson?"

"If you mean do I know the difference between love and lust, yes I do.

She glanced his way before turning the key in the ignition.

"Care to explain?"

Wulf was not sure if he could tell Raven in words how he knew and why he knew. He just knew it had something to do with her. The way she stood up to him, the way she welcomed his kisses and touch, the way she smiled when he did something strange for her time period.

"I be not sure I can, but I be sure that if I had not met you, I would still be puzzling it out in my head."

Her blue eyes went wide for a moment, and for the first time since they had met, his little… No, when did she become his Raven? Wulf was at a loss for words.

When the silence stretched on, she finally shook her head. "Alrighty then…I guess we should get you something to eat before we head back home." Her hands clenched the turning wheel in the car, and she pulled out onto the street.

All during the time they stopped for food and waited to pick it up, she avoided looking his way.

He clenched his own fists. He wanted to see her eyes. Could she tell from his words that he cared about her? Did she know he found her the most desirable woman he had ever met?

No. Because he be too much of a coward to tell her. What good would it do? Sooner or later, Catriona would send him back to his time, and Raven would dwell in a future he would never visit again. His bones would be nothing but dust in a grave before the year 2010 arrived and she would be left, if he was blessed, with a memory of him. But did he have the right to make her hurt (if she cared for him) for an indefinite amount of time?

And did he have the right to bed her only to leave her possibly with child? There was no way he could know when or if he might be jerked back to Norseland, but he could not take that chance. The thought of a child he might never see would shatter his already aching heart.

Somehow, somewhere, he'd fallen hard for the little writer.

"We're home. Are you going to sit there all afternoon or come in?"

Wrapped up in his thoughts, he had not realized they arrived back at her home, nor did he even know when Raven left the car. Now as he looked at her through the glass on his side, he wondered what he was going to do. How would he keep his hands from touching her, his lips from kissing her, and his traitorous body from claiming what he knew should be his?

He gathered his thoughts, harnessed his courage, and rebuked his body. "Sorry, aye, I be getting out."

Wulf ignored the slight smile she passed his way and sidestepped the hand she put out to him.

"I guess we can watch a movie if you like after we eat." Her hesitant words made him want to gather her to him, but he did not. So despondent over what he couldn't or wouldn't do, he didn't even ask what a movie was.

****

Seated at the kitchen table, Raven slapped a couple of pieces of pizza on a paper plate and handed it to Wulf. The man had not uttered a word for over thirty minutes, except for the few brief words when they arrived home. Not at all like the inquisitive wonder she was becoming to care about way more than she should.

Still, they couldn't just not talk to one another—he could be here for a long time. Of course, she could put him up at a hotel, but her heart just wasn't in it.

"Okay, out with it. You seemed fine earlier today, and now you've clammed up like a hooker in church. What's wrong?"

His silver eyes darkened to almost black as he finished chewing the bite of pizza in his mouth, and then wiped his lips on a napkin.

"You mean besides my being here in the wrong century with you? Adrift from all I know, destined to maybe never seeing my homeland again?"

Hurt slapped Raven in the face and then traveled inside to attack her heart. Sure, the man had a right to be agitated, but his angst at being in the wrong century included her. The woman who had taken him in, the woman he'd kissed senseless, the woman who didn't understand why he couldn't love her the way she was beginning to love him.

Whoa, don't go there, you know this can't happen. You've already had this conversation with yourself.

"Look Wulf, I'm sorry. I can't tell you I understand how you feel, but try to understand how

I feel. I thought we were beginning to be friends, maybe a bit more, and now you berate and ignore me like I was a stranger."

"What would you rather I do? Take you to bed and give you a babe? For that could happen and then when Catriona whirls me back to my time, you will be left alone."

Well, what they said about great minds and all that drivel was on the mark. They both had been thinking about his leaving. Raven wondered if Wulf would miss her when he left. She doubted it. He had so many women wanting his body, and she'd be just an inconsequential memory.

The rest of their meal turned into a silent struggle to eat and not look at one another. Not what she wanted, or planned, but she wasn't sure she could or wanted to change Wulf's mind.

When Wulf didn't break the silence, and her courage failed her too much to do it either, Raven pushed back her chair and began to collect the remains of their half-eaten meal. The Viking must be stressed. He'd left food on his plate, something she had not seen since he first became her house guest.

"Look, I'm going to grab a shower. You know how to turn on the television set, right?"

"Aye! I be not ignorant."

"Fine, then find something to watch."

Tears blurred her eyes at his harsh words as Raven made her way into her bedroom. His words hurt. And even though he might be upset himself, it still didn't give him the right to bite the hand that was feeding, clothing, and bedding him down.

Whoops, bedding was not the best word to use. It brought up all kinds of delicious and forbidden thoughts. She stripped off her clothes and headed to the bathroom. The shrill piping of her cell phone from the den disrupted her thoughts.

She spun around just as the bedroom door

opened.

Chapter Six

Wulf stood in the doorway. The look on his face changed from stony-eyed angst to a smoldering silver fire.

Shocked at his sudden appearance, the gown she still held in her hands fell to her feet.

The Viking's expression burned hotter as he took a step forward. His action spurred Raven into motion. She grabbed the gown and anchored the material to her body. Her hands trembled from more than being startled.

She waited to see what Wulf's next move would be.

Raven didn't have to wait long.

The Viking surged forward as if he were in battle, caught her body in his arms, and pulled her close.

"Woman, you would try the patience of a saint, and I be not one."

Wulf's lips captured Raven's, and he basked in the welcome he received. The image of her naked body burned in his mind and shaft. Thor's hammer, he knew she was a buxom wench, but never would he have thought her body would be the enticement most men could only dream of.

And thank the Valkyries she did not deny entrance to his lips or tongue. He removed one of his hands from around her waist and pulled the material she used as a shield away from her luscious body. Now, both his hands cupped and lightly tested the weight of her impressive breasts.

His action spurred a groan from Raven, which he captured and returned to her with foraging sweeps of his tongue.

With such bounty before him, Wulf hesitated to leave the nectar of her rosy peaks, but he craved to explore the treasure hidden within the blonde hair between her thighs.

Nay, 'twas not all he wanted to do, but for now he would satisfy his curiosity if the silken pelt was as soft as his quick glance told him it would be.

Raven moaned when Wulf's hand slid down the outside of her thigh, and then up the inside. His fingertips were a bit calloused, but his touch was gentle as well as seductive.

His thumb found and trapped the core of her desire and her knees buckled. Raven found herself on the floor with Wulf lying almost on top of her. A discordant sound coming from his shirt pocket broke her lust-filled thoughts.

"Raven, what are you doing? I need to talk to you right now!"

For a moment, she thought she'd lost her mind until she spied her cell phone riding almost out of Wulf's shirt.

Caroline! Oh, pish! That was the reason Wulf came into her bedroom in the first place. She made a grab for the phone before it slid onto the floor and stuck it to her ear—all the time telling her body to shut up as it screamed for more.

"Wulf, get off of me." Her whisper met with an icy glare and then a subtle but definite look of hurt.

Raven gained her feet right after the Viking did.

"Raven!"

"I'm here, Caroline, what is it?"

"Your deadline's been moved up. What took you so long to come to the phone? And who is the guy that answered it in the first place?"

She didn't have to see her editor's face to know her brows were pulled up in a frown, or her nose was tilted slightly up in the air as she waited for an answer.

"Well..."

"Well what?"

"Wulf is a friend, he needed a place to stay."

Her words sounded just as defensive as she felt.

"Oh, and is this the same guy that stirred up all kinds of sin-filled thoughts at the book signing?"

"I guess it was too much to expect that Lillian and Maxine would keep their mouths shut."

"Honey, he brought in a crowd you haven't seen in a bit."

Raven wanted to slap-kick Caroline. So what? Sales had been down just a bit, but in today's economy, that was to be expected.

"I think you should keep him around, at least until your next book goes best-seller. Which reminds me..."

Okay, finally the reason Caroline really called for.

"I need your book finished in the next two weeks."

Raven watched with a sinking heart and unsatisfied body as Wulf strode from her room. Should she call him back? His face pretty much said it all. He was incensed and hurt. But what else could she do?

She had to take this call and if she examined her feelings closer, she knew, as much as she wanted him, it was better this way. She had bigger fish to fry than bedding a Viking, even if her body still wept from wanting him. The best thing she could do for Wulf would be to make sure whoever was targeting her did not get a chance to take it out on him. And she needed to finish writing her freaking book before Caroline had a conniption fit.

"Are you listening, Raven?"

"Yes, I heard you loud and clear. I'll get the book to you. Now, if there's nothing else, I have something I need to do."

Her editor's husky laugh came through the cell

phone. "I just bet you do. Just make sure Mr. Hunk-of-Sin doesn't destroy your concentration. I need the manuscript in two weeks."

"Don't worry, you'll have it." It might be rude, but Raven closed her cell phone without giving her editor a chance to say anything else.

Against her heart's cry for her to do something different, Raven closed the door Wulf left open when he stalked out and took her shower. Only when her body was safely shrouded with flannel, all the makeup off her face from the afternoon, and her hair pulled up in a tight and hurtful knot on top of her head did she leave her room.

The den was dark, no sounds of the television. He must have gone to his room. Her slippered foot tapped as she tried to decide whether to go back and hide in her room or beard the Viking in his cave.

Honor won out over cowardice. She owed him an apology. Yes, she did need to talk to Caroline, but there were better ways she could have handled the situation.

Her steps were slow as she walked to the guest room, her hand hesitant as she finally tapped on the door.

Silence met her knock. Raven waited a full thirty seconds and repeated her action. Still nothing.

"Wulf? Are you awake? I want to talk to you."

Nothing. She was ready to turn around and go back to her room when she heard a slight grunt and then a harsh, clipped voice. "Leave me be, Raven. I want no more of your talking or anything else."

Pain shot through her heart, but she remained silent as she retraced her steps. Only when she was safely inside her room with the door locked, did she give in to the tears burning her eyes.

Chapter Seven

Wulf punched his pillow, rolled over, and closed his eyes, but nothing helped. He'd been awake for what seemed like hours. He wanted to kick his own arse for snapping at Raven. Why did he not try to talk to her? He knew why, but did not want to admit his shaft had overcome his mind.

His first glimpse of her total nudity had turned his legs into storm-tossed twigs. His manhood had worked fine, standing up like a sword, and nothing Wulf did would stop the lust making it harder than a ship's mast.

When she'd turned into his embrace and returned his kiss, he forgot about handing her the little box she talked into. He did not recall his decision to not touch Raven, nor his troublesome thoughts about leaving her.

All he could think about was touching her, making her his, never allowing her out of his arms again. Living in this time was very different than his. At home, all he would have to do was claim her before witnesses and he could bed her all he wanted. She would be his. Here, women held jobs, walked around in men's clothing, and did what they wanted.

Yet, they still needed to be revered. They were the givers of life to children. And the Christian God help him, he wanted children for the first time in his life. He wanted to hold a child that belonged to him and Raven.

His eyes burned from the emotion tugging at his heart. If this be love, then Catriona had gotten her revenge. His heart ached with the knowledge that he could not make Raven his wife. Even if she were of a like mind, and even if there were a way for her to return home with him, he could never ask her to leave the life she was used to.

Nay, Raven's halt of their lovemaking was for the best. Now, he would need to keep his love and lust in control.

On that thought, he rolled over onto his stomach in an effort to quiet the lust attacking his shaft.

****

Raven crept through the house and hoped Wulf was a heavy sleeper. She'd not seen any sign of him when she got up to make coffee. Even after getting dressed, silence still reigned in the guest room.

Whether or not he was indeed asleep, or plain ignoring her, she was grateful. After tossing and turning for most of the night, she'd retrieved the note and decided to take it and the picture she'd printed out from the cemetery to the police station. Maybe someone there could help her.

****

"Yes, I'd like to speak to Sergeant Giles please." Raven placed the note on the counter and waited.

"Sorry, ma'am, he's out on patrol. Maybe someone else could help you." The officer at the front desk gave her a slight smile and went back to pushing paperwork to the side of the desk.

"Possibly, who would I talk to about a—" Before she could get the word "threat" out, chaos broke loose in the station. A man in handcuffs started yelling and then began head butting the officer escorting him.

Several men in blue jumped in to try and subdue the prisoner. Raven opened her mouth to ask the officer at the desk who she could talk to, but he too dove into the fracas.

What should she do? Wait? Leave? What? The prisoner himself helped make up her mind when he grabbed a letter opener off one of the desks and started slicing the air with it.

****

Too much of a chicken to go home and face Wulf's cold demeanor, Raven decided to go to the bookstore and stock up on some of her favorite authors. Just maybe she'd be alive to enjoy the vampire romances. Besides, she was *so* not in the mood to meet her book deadline. She also needed to make a stop at the grocery store. So far all she'd offered Wulf to eat was fast food. Tonight she would cook for him, and with the extra stuff she'd thrown in her cart, maybe he wouldn't starve if she didn't make it home tonight.

Now, several hours later, she inserted her key in the front door lock and juggled two bags of groceries as well as a carton of cola.

Before she could push the door open, it was snatched backward.

"Where have you been?" Wulf's snarl caused Raven to jump back, almost dropping the groceries.

"I had some things to do."

"You did not tell me you would be leaving." This time his tone smacked of a little boy's pout.

"If you'll step back so I can get in, I might tell you what I was doing." Raven blew a lock of hair out of her eyes and then stepped over the threshold when Wulf moved.

"And just so you know," she intoned over her shoulder as she made for the kitchen, "I don't have to tell you when I leave."

" 'Tis rude and you know it."

"Fine, you want to fight about me not leaving a note, let's do it, but I'd like to know why you stormed out last night."

"I will not talk about that with you." Wulf's lips tightened into a straight, uncompromising line.

"Fine, then I don't want to talk to you."

Raven began to put up the groceries, turning her back on the Viking male who needed an attitude adjustment.

When she turned back around, he was gone.

"Fine, arrogant piece of medieval pig."

****

Raven chopped onions and peppers to add to the ground beef simmering on the stove. She hoped Wulf liked chili, and she hoped he started talking to her. Silence pretty much had been her companion since their earlier heated discussion. Another *thwack*, *thwack* with her knife and she tossed the green, white, and red pieces into the skillet to cook with the meat.

The can opener swirled, and she poured in a can of tomatoes and stirred the spicy mixture. Before she opened the fridge to get the salad fixings, she stepped into the hallway. Not a sound reached her from Wulf's room. The man was good and steamed. Her anger over his words dissipated right after he stormed away—leaving behind a crushing ache in her heart.

Yes, she knew what she was doing was for the best, for Wulf's sake, but it still bit big time. She finished the final touches on the salad, tasted the chili to make sure all the spices were blended, and then got down plates and bowls. Not much for cooking unless she had to, her lifestyle commanded fast food more times than not, Raven opted to pick up a dessert at the grocery store. Brownies with cream cheese icing should go far, she hoped, to sweeten the Viking's attitude.

Twenty minutes later, she stood outside his doorway and knocked. "Wulf, it's time to eat."

"I not be hungry."

"Please, I know you are upset with me, but can't we talk over dinner?" Raven knew her words held a plea within them, but she didn't much care if she sounded like she was begging. Dusk was only about two hours off, and she wanted to spend some time with Wulf. There were things he needed to know if something happened to her. Of course, she was an idiot for going back to the cemetery in the first place, but she couldn't take a chance on another break-in with Wulf as the target.

The door opened quietly, a good sign, but the scowl on his handsome face prepared her for the battle ahead. She'd be blessed if she could get him to listen to anything she had to say.

"Great, thanks for coming out."

His grunt didn't help her confidence as he slid past her, keeping a good foot of distance between their bodies. Sheesh, when the man pouted, he pouted all the way.

Once they were seated with plates of salad and bowls of chili decorating the place mats, Raven tried once again to break though his rotten mood. "Wulf, look I know I said I wasn't going to talk about last night. Yes, it did not turn out like I wanted it to, but you have to understand, I have to work. It's just me, and if I can't make a living, I have no one else to help."

She watched his strong jaw clench as he chewed a forkful of salad and then waited until he swallowed. His silver gaze speared her like he'd speared a piece of tomato out of his salad.

"Well, aren't you going to say anything?"

Wulf finished the tomato, laid his fork down, and picked up the can of cola. His Adam's apple worked as he downed a good bit of the liquid before he set the can down.

"I'm sorry." The apology came out in a gruff tone, but the metallic cast to his beautiful eyes had softened.

Raven felt the burn start in the back of her eyes. She did not want to cry, but she never expected him to say he was sorry. Not at all sure what she thought might happen, she could only return his look before she could open her mouth to reply.

"I'm sorry too. I know if I were you, I'd be scared out of my mind being so far from all I know. You are so brave, and I should have been more understanding."

" 'Tis probably not easy on you either." The half-smile on his lips warmed her insides.

"No, but I'm learning to cope. Although, having you barge into my bedroom last night was a bit hard to handle."

Wulf's laughter filled the kitchen and went straight to Raven's heart. In the short time since they had met, this was the first time he actually laughed out loud.

"What's so funny, Viking?"

When he controlled his amusement, he finally answered her question.

"You may think me seeing you in your birthing suit was hard, but it cannot compare to the hardness I experienced."

Heat blossomed in her cheeks and climbed toward her forehead, almost scalding her skin. She remembered the hardness of his body, the masculine weight of his arousal as he lay over her body on the floor. Truth be known, she wanted that hardness inside her. Embedded so deeply he could never leave.

"I, uh, guess I should say I'm sorry again. Just so you know, I ached also."

Wulf stood up and then rounded the table where he crouched down next to Raven.

"Then why did you tell the woman on your talking box I was just a friend?"

Raven thought long and hard about her words. If she allowed him to know her heart, then both she and him would be hurt when he left. Not to mention, the simple fact she might not be around. Stupid, stupid, not to have waited around for Sergeant Giles. Now it was too late to do anything.

"Because that is all we can ever be. I'm sure know that already. Without knowing how long you will be here, it would be foolish to try and make this relationship more than it is."

"And what is it?"

"Two people who met and will be parting sometime."

The words cut her almost as much as the look on Wulf's face. The hurt in his eyes turned them a molten silver before he wiped all expression from his gaze.

"You be right, there is nothing for you or me in this time. Catriona could call me back at any given moment. 'Tis best we do not engage in anything other than acquaintances."

The monotone of his sentences made her wonder if Wulf told the truth. Did it matter? He was right as was she. Nothing could be between them.

"Good, I'm glad we have an understanding. Now, I'm going to clean up in here and then I have to go out."

"Out? 'Tis almost night."

"Well, women in this time do go out without an escort, so while I clean, there are a few things you need to know."

****

Wulf watched Raven drive off. Her explanation she needed to run an errand did not sit well with him. He might be from another time, but he was well versed in knowing when someone was up to something. She would not look him in the eyes when he asked her where she was going, and she almost swooned when he asked if he could go with her. The sun was just beginning to set when he stepped out onto the front of Raven's house. His movements were agitated as he stomped back and forth.

He didn't know why, but he had a bad feeling about her leaving. Her directions on what to do if something happened to her were almost frantic. That he could live in her house as long as he needed to. If he needed any money or groceries, he should go to her agent and she would take care of it. As if she didn't think she would get back home safely.

Thor's hammer, he should have insisted that he go with her.

A purring sound came down the drive and what he now knew was a car came to a stop. One of the policemen who came and took away the offal who attacked Raven climbed out of the metal box.

"Is Ms. Harrison here?" He asked the question at the same time he stuck his hand out to shake Wulf's.

"No, Raven left just a few moments ago."

The man looked at his watch and then up at the darkening sky. "We need to get to the cemetery."

Chapter Eight

"What's wrong?" Wulf's heart accelerated with the tight, near-anxious look on the man's face.

"If I'm right, Ms. Harrison could be in danger."

This time his heart skipped several beats before it settled back into a somewhat booming rhythm.

"Let's go."

"Sir, it could be dangerous, you need to stay here. Besides the note made reference..." His words trailed off as he looked up at Wulf.

"The note?"

"The one she received yesterday morning. The same one she left at the police station today."

Wulf did not know what to say or think. Raven had not trusted him enough to tell him about the note.

"What did the note say?" His question came out more as a demand than an inquiry. The man who turned to get back in his car, paused before answering.

"A note pretty much threatening your life, taking credit for the break-in here, the night before last, and the threat implied Ms. Harrison needed to bring her camera and come alone."

The explanation told Wulf why Raven had acted in some of the ways she had earlier.

"Why would the note writer involve me? I have only been here for a few days."

"Well, you were at the cemetery when the shots were fired, and you were here when they tried to kill Ms. Harrison. Undoubtedly they are using you to force her to do what they want."

Rage tore a path through Wulf's head and then

body. His fists clenched and unclenched with the desire to kill. He'd heard of Vikings becoming berserkers in the midst of battle, but he'd always kept that part locked up. Raven being in danger was the key to unleashing that curse.

"We have to get there and protect her," he growled.

"I agree, but you need to stay here. It will only muddy the waters if the man sees you."

"We will make sure he does not see me, for I will not be left behind." He didn't know if the man saw the determination in his expression or just didn't want to waste time arguing, but he nodded his head.

"All right, get in. We'll go up the back entrance to the cemetery. Tell me again where you first heard the shots."

Wulf closed the door to the car. "Near a tall building on a hill."

"Sound's like the Tanner family mausoleum."

He didn't care how they got there as long as they got there before something happened to Raven.

****

Raven cautiously walked up the hill to the mausoleum. Before she left home, she'd stuck a knife inside the cuff of her boot, and made sure her pepper spray was stashed securely inside her waistband, hidden by her jacket.

On the drive over she'd come to the decision, the creep threatening her and Wulf would not go unscathed if he tried anything. With the lack of police assistance, she was on her own.

Which is your own fault. Shut up! she told the voice inside her head. No way could she bring Wulf into this mess. No matter if he never forgave her for freezing him out. She was doing it for his own good.

The sky hung like a dark specter over her head. Only one decorative light worked on the path. The weak beam did nothing to penetrate the darkness, or to make her feel even a bit safer.

"That's far enough." A rough voice came from a few feet ahead just as Raven finished the climb.

"Look, I'm here. I've got the camera, and I just want to get this over with." Raven hoped her voice sounded stronger than the rest of her body felt.

"That's good. I see you also came alone." This time the voice evolved into a face and body.

"I followed your directions."

"Yes, you did. Now hand me the camera."

Raven unhooked the camera from around her neck, but didn't put it in the man's outstretched hand.

"If I give it to you, what reassurance do I have you won't try to hurt Wulf?"

"Wulf...ah yes, the boyfriend. Well, if I were you, I would be more worried about yourself."

His tone of voice struck a chord of terror inside her trembling body. She should have thought this through some more. What if he didn't just let her go?

Duh? She'd already thought of that scenario, and she'd come prepared. If she died, at least the world would know what happened. She eased her hand slightly to the pocket of her jacket and pressed. The soft whirl of the mini recorder reassured her at least her death would be on record, and the scumbag would not go free.

"Look, I don't even know you, so let's just get this over with. You can go your way and I'll go mine."

"I don't think so. Sooner or later, you will hear about the embezzling going on at Masterson and Dean. Of course, if my partner had not caught me, then I wouldn't have had to kill him." He paused as if considering something. "I should have used a knife, like tonight, but then I wouldn't have been able to shoot at you and your friend."

The man stepped farther out from the shadow of the building. His tall frame dwarfed hers, and the deep blue of his eyes carried only menace. He swiped a lock of brown hair away from his face.

"So you see, it doesn't matter if you know me now, and please don't take it personally, but I do have to kill you."

Raven's heart stopped for a moment, until she realized she didn't want to die. Not here, not now.

"I'll make it easy. Just a quick stab to your heart and it'll be over. I already have a grave ready for you. The one I dug for my partner is plenty big enough for two. And the good thing is, the headstone belongs to someone else. No way will the police associate it with your death, if they ever find out about your early demise."

"I don't suppose you would believe me if I said I wouldn't tell anyone."

His laugh rasped across her spine. Evil did not describe the tone.

"Hardly, and I would not rule out the possibility you've already uploaded the photos to your computer. Besides, I have found I like killing. Too bad your friend did not come with you."

"Yeah, well, if he had you wouldn't stand a chance."

"What a shame we won't find out."

Raven waited as he moved closer. Her body, although, she remained upright, still readied itself to defend herself. He moved closer.

Come on, you arrogant oaf. Let's see you take me out without a fight.

The knife he carried gleamed for just a moment as the moon chose to come out and then run and hide.

It was enough she could see he held it in the downward position to strike. Her pepper spray caressed her palm, and she eased off the safety so she could spray the son-of-a—

The knife slashed down so quickly, Raven could do nothing but stand there for all of one second. She brought up the can of spray, spritzed the man good, and then slammed him with her camera.

He went down like a rock. She refused the strong urge to kick him in the family jewels. He looked as if he was out like a light. Probably broke her camera in the bargain.

"Ms. Harrison?"

Raven turned to fight a possible new threat. Her relief escaped in a breath of air.

"Raven?" Wulf's question did all kinds of marvelous things to her body. He sounded like he cared. How and why he was here (not to mention Detective Giles) didn't matter. She was saved, the bad guy could go to jail, and hopefully, just maybe, she and Wulf could sort out what type of relationship they might hope to have while he remained in her time.

"Are you all right?"

"Yes, Detective, but how did you find me?"

"You forgot the note from Mr. Dean."

"Who?"

"The man you took out on your own. We got here to hear most of the conversation but I didn't want to startle the man, so we waited." Giles' explanation sounded plausible, but for the life of her she still didn't know Dean from a squirrel in her front yard.

Wulf moved close to Raven. "You never answered me. Are you all right?" His concern touched her heart deep inside. The frown that marred his handsome face worried her.

"I'm fine, Wulf. Now that we've caught the bad guy."

Detective Giles broke in. "From where I'm standing, Ms. Harrison, you did all the work yourself."

For some reason, the detective's smile and approval made Raven uncomfortable. His words certainly did nothing to erase the storm cloud gathering on Wulf's countenance.

"I got lucky, and the pepper spray did most of

the work."

She moved a bit closer to the Viking. "So what happens now, does the guy go to jail for murder?"

"Yes, we got a tip from his partner, Noel James, a few weeks ago. Too bad Mr. James decided to take on Waters himself. He had a wife and child."

"That's horrible." Raven's voice shook with the realization she could have been in the grave with the dead man.

"So, I guess now the family can at least know what happened."

"Yes. Thanks to you." Detective Giles handcuffed Dean and then shook hands with both her and Wulf.

"I'll follow you back to your house and maybe you can put this all behind you."

"Yes, ah, I have the pictures of him standing over a body; they're not that clear, but you are welcome to them."

"Great, that should help make this even more of an airtight case."

Chapter Nine

Wulf listened to Raven and the policeman exchange pleasantries after they arrived back at her house. He remained silent. The core of fear that assaulted him when the detective told him about Raven's secretive meeting still trapped him in its grip, but it was only half of what he felt.

After watching the knife almost strike Raven, he began to think fear was not strong enough to describe the emotion shaking his insides. Terror, panic, dread caused his hands to tremble.

The other emotions were self-loathing and rage. He should have been there to protect Raven. He should have been there to kill the man who attacked her. Instead, he stood by like a stone while she saved herself.

He was a warrior, a man, a jarl of his own people and yet he did nothing to help the woman he loved. *Loved?* His heart stuttered with the acknowledgment. When it happened, he didn't know, but he was certain of it when he thought Raven would be lost to him.

He clenched his fists until they ached. She was already lost to him. Catriona would never favor him with love. With all he had done in the past, she would probably flaunt his deeds and then send him back to the past so fast, he would not even get to say goodbye.

"Well, I think we're finished, Ms. Harrison. You two have a good night."

"Thanks, and you have a safe one." Raven waved. "Come on, Wulf. I am so glad to be home!" Her joy melted some of his morass but not enough.

Once inside, she moved toward the kitchen. He lagged behind. If he had any sense about him, he would just take her in his arms, make love to her, and then cherish the memory.

The old Wulf would have, but the man he was now would honor their agreement.

"Hey, you coming? I've got a bottle of champagne somewhere in one of these cabinets, and I plan on popping the cork. I am so glad this is over!"

Only after he held a glass of the unfamiliar bubbly liquid and they had drank to the fact Raven was alive, did he finally voice the briar rubbing him raw.

"Raven, why did you not tell me about the note?"

Raven took another sip of champagne and thought long and hard over what she could say.

"I, uh, didn't tell you because I was afraid you would get—"

"Do not tell me you feared I would be hurt!" His roar almost deafened her.

"Wulf, you are just a man, and you don't even have the weapons you carried back in your time."

"Did you not think I could protect you without a weapon? I learned also to fight with my hands, my body."

Raven took one peek at his smoldering gaze and looked away.

"Look at me, Raven. To deny me the chance to protect you is to doubt me as a man."

Snapping her head up to glare at him, she commanded, "Wait just one minute. What I did has nothing to do with you being a man. It was doing what was prudent."

"Truly? You actually believe going out to confront a man who has tried to kill you before was wise?" Wulf shoved away from the table and stalked around the kitchen.

Raven took another sip of champagne before setting the glass on the table. "Look, I never thought about it hurting your feelings. I'm sorry."

"An apology does not make it right. You could have been killed." His words slashed an arc of anger deep inside Raven.

She did it to protect him. No matter the man was stupid and did not realize what could have happened. Waters could have used a gun like he did before. Wulf was no more equipped to handle that type of weaponry…well, than she was. Oh Lord, no wonder he thought she didn't think him man enough.

All the time they had been together, she'd been protecting him. It probably did something to his male psyche.

Raven stood up and moved toward Wulf. She placed a hand on his arm to prevent him from pacing. He shook it off.

"Look, I said I was sorry. I just didn't think. I care about you and didn't want you to get hurt."

A deep breath escaped his lips. "Did you not think I felt the same way? In my time, we protect our women. For you to stop me from doing that makes me feel useless, Raven."

"But this is not your time. Women can protect themselves here, and even though it's sweet you want to take care of me, it's not always going to happen. You're going back to your time. We just don't know when."

"I can—"

"Yes, you can protect me while you're here, but I need to be aware myself of what can happen. Lord knows, I hope I never have another experience like I've had for the last couple of days, present company excluded, but if God forbid I have to protect myself, then I can't wait on you or anyone else to do it. Do you understand?"

"Aye, you do not want or need me to protect you."

"That's not what I said and you know it."

Wulf's eyes darkened, and the growl he pulsed into the air caused Raven to step back.

"By not telling me what was going on, you did just that."

Now her dander was up. "You know, I don't care. I've tried to placate your oversized ego. Tried to make you feel at home away from home, and I've tried to keep in mind, no matter how much I want you physically, it's not going to happen." She followed her words with one step forward and then another. "So, how about this. If you don't like what's going on, then just bloody well leave!"

She wasn't sure who was more surprised at her ultimatum, her or Wulf. Regardless, he didn't leave her long in wondering what he would do.

"I believe that would be for the best. I will be leaving come morning."

For the life of her, Raven couldn't stop the words from running out of her mouth. "Why wait until morning. Why not go now?"

"If 'tis what you wish." Wulf's silver gleam dulled. She didn't want to know what emotion caused it, she told herself, she didn't care.

"Yes, 'tis what I wish," she mimicked. "Viking, go home!" The yell punctuating her sentence was totally not Raven's normal behavior, but the words she mumbled under her breath said it all, "Before I lose my freaking mind as well as my heart."

****

Wulf let himself out the front door and started walking. The night had grown colder since they got home from the cemetery. Storm clouds gathered far off, but would move into the area before dawn from the way it looked. He should have changed back into his braies and left the clothing Raven brought him with her.

He didn't want or need anything from the woman.

Liar!

He wanted what he couldn't have. His shoulders slumped just a bit. He really had no idea where to go. Without the plastic Raven used as coin, he'd have to sleep where he could find a spot. Funny how being in this century had spoiled him just a bit with the creature comforts.

He would miss the wondrous miracle of inside baths. Although, he would not miss Raven's constant harping. Her mother had named her aptly. The cawing and screeching had worn out his welcome in his opinion.

Women! You do what you think they want and still land in a mess. 'Twas a dark day or night when he found himself falling head over sword for Raven. Sure he could talk himself into believing 'twas not love, but sooner or later the truth would come out.

Wulf stopped for a moment. His direction had taken him away from what Raven called streets toward a copse of trees and what looked like a meadow. With the night heralding rain, he would find shelter under or in a tree until morning. After that, he was uncertain where he would go.

Once settled against a tree trunk, he closed his eyes. Only then would he allow himself to think about what his life would be like without Raven. Surely, Catriona had it right. Love was a vast cry from just dipping his shaft into any willing body. For the most part, he forgot the women he bedded come the next morning. He'd not even taken Raven completely and all he could think about was how he loved lying by her side and just watching her sleep.

'Twas a veritable grave he'd dug for himself.

A slight sound woke Wulf from his light sleep. He opened his eyes to the iridescent glow of lights. Before he could gain his feet, one light, a rich purple, separated from the other colors and floated toward him.

His heart faltered for a moment until he realized the light began to spin into the shape of a woman.

Catriona!

What he had hoped for had come to pass, but now he was not sure he wanted it.

"Well, Viking, this isn't where I thought I would find you."

Wulf decided to show no fear of the faery princess.

"And just where did you think I would be? It is not as if I knew anyone in this age when you popped me to the future."

Catriona's eyes darkened to a darker shade of emerald. Her brows pulled into a frown, and her lips opened to emit a shrill, but thank the Gods short, essence of sound.

"Do not displease me, Wulfgar. I had hoped to keep this to a pleasant conversation."

"Pleasant? Is that possible?" Wulf growled back.

For some reason his question amused her. Catriona's laughter resembled tinkling bells in the wind.

"Yes, now if you would refrain from speaking, I will tell you why I'm here."

He kept his lips tightly closed. The allure of saying something she would probably turn him into a frog for was strong. Wulf nodded his head.

"Good. I will admit when I sent you to this year, I truly felt you would die in this time. I did not see how you would ever separate the meaning of love and lust." Catriona smiled.

"To say it was a unexpected surprise would not even state the obvious, but I am pleased with what has conspired. You indeed know the difference, and your restraint in not taking Raven to bed as you wanted is admirable."

Catriona waved her hand and plucked a silk scarf from the air before dusting off a tree stump near where Wulf sat. "I also know you lost your heart to her early on but the emotion only fermented your brain when she was almost killed."

Wulf's air ejected when he opened his mouth to speak." How do you know this?"

Catriona lifted one shoulder in an elegant shrug. "I'm of the Fey, we know more than mortals do. I also know you left her because she didn't need your help."

" 'Tis not true."

"I sense a lie, Viking. You were exceedingly upset. What I don't understand is why."

Wulf drew his brows together in a scowl. "Why? Because 'tis my place to look after Raven."

"Well, that is something that will have to change if you love her."

"You make no sense, Princess. What love we have will do neither of us any good when you send me home."

"As you say, but I could return you to your home and send Raven with you."

"You would do this?" His heart jumped at the thought he could keep her, but it quickly faded to a onerous beat. He would not ask Raven to return to his time. Even if she willed it so, he would not take her away from what she knew.

"Aye, but you pretty much ruined your chances with her, unless you go back and talk to her. Male pride should not stand in the way of true love."

He eyed Catriona with skepticism. "And you know this because?"

"Let us just say, male faeries can be stubborn also. Now get going and call for me when you have the answer."

Before Wulf could say anything else, Catriona surprised him when she leaned over, kissed him on the cheek, and then disappeared.

Strange she be, woman or faerie. He ignored the slight chill slithering up his back as he listened to the tinkling sound of laughter. At least she had given him something to think about. Should he stay here in the present or go home? Should he go by himself or ask Raven to go with him?

Chapter Ten

Raven ran back the way she'd come. She'd waited and waited for Wulf to come back. After all, he didn't really know anyone here but her. Surely he would return before it got too late.

After several hours crawled by, she'd rode around trying to find him. Ready to give up, a flash of light near a wooded area caught her attention. Leaving her car, she'd crept toward the still-shimmering mist and found Wulf.

Wulf and a beautiful woman!

She couldn't hear their conversation but she certainly did not miss the kiss. So much for worrying about him being somewhere cold and alone.

Tears blurred her vision as she made it back to her car and climbed in. She was right to tell him to go home. It seemed his hurt feelings had been soothed.

The Viking was out of her life and that was a good thing!

Is it?

Shut up! she mouthed back to her inner voice. She didn't need a stinking man in her life. She had and would continue to make it on her own.

A few minutes later, she pulled into her driveway. A couple of moments more and she locked the front door behind her.

She allowed her body to slide down the hard wood until she huddled on the floor. Only then did she give in to the heartache tearing her soul apart.

A while later she scrubbed away the last of her crying jag with her knuckles. Life had to go on and she would survive. She'd been fine before she met

Wulf, and she would again. It might take a bit of time, but...

"Raven." Her name on Wulf's lips caused her to sit up straight. The pounding on her front door galvanized her into action.

What did he want?

"Raven!"

"Go away, Wulf." She was proud her voice did not quake.

"I need to talk to you. Now, woman. Open the door."

The command in his voice set off warning bells inside Raven. Something had his back up, but what? He should be happy. If the woman she spied him with was the elusive Catriona, then he should be yelling his joy.

"There is nothing to talk about. You don't need me, so go home."

A full minute of silence passed between them before Wulf growled, "You have no idea what you speak of, Raven. Now open this damn door before I break it down."

Afraid he would do exactly what he threatened, and hurt himself in the bargain, Raven unbolted the door.

Before she could tell him to go away again, she was caught in a pair of arms that almost squeezed the daylights out of her.

"I can't breathe, Wulf. Let go."

"I be sorry, Raven, but I have tidings."

Once his arms released their hold, Raven stepped back over the threshold. Wulf followed her into the house.

"I don't suppose this has anything to do with the blonde kissing you, does it?"

His facial features looked stunned, but he recovered quickly. "You saw her?"

"Yes."

"Good. Did you hear what she said?

"No. I got there in time to see her kiss you."

" 'Twas strange, that kiss. I don't know why she did so."

"Are you sure? From where I watched, it looked as if she was more than taken with you. It makes me wonder if she banished you for an entirely different reason than you told me. Perhaps she was jealous?"

Wulf's laughter was unwelcome.

Raven drew herself up to her full height. "I don't find anything funny about any of this, Wulf. I told you to go home, and I meant it."

" 'Tis not what ye think. Catriona kissed me on the cheek."

"Yeah, right!"

" 'Tis true, I want no other woman kissing me but you, Raven. Now listen to what I'm trying to tell you. Princess Catriona says I may return home. She also said you could come with me."

"Yeah, like I'm into threesomes. I don't think so."

"Threesome?" Wulf's brows drew together for a moment. "There is and would never be a threesome. I love only you, Raven. "Don't you love me?"

His question threw her off stride. Yes, she did love him, but his entire fabrication that she could go with him was ludicrous.

"Even if I do, what makes you think I want to go back to medieval times or beyond? I have a life here. Maybe I don't want to give it up."

"Raven, I love you. I want you to go with me, but if you will not, then I will stay here."

Raven forced her weak legs to head for the den. She found a perch on the sofa and then took several deep breaths.

"I can't let you do that. You have responsibilities back home."

"But I cannot—"

A bright light filled the room. Raven shuttered her eyes to keep them from hurting. When she reopened them, the blonde stood in the room.

Having only seen her profile before, she wasn't prepared for the beauty the Princess Catriona radiated. No wonder Wulf was in awe of the faery.

"Enough, mortal woman. I have listened to you and Wulfgar battle back and forth until it hurts my ears."

She moved closer to Raven. "You have done what I feared no woman would be able to do—make the Viking fall in love with you."

Raven opened her mouth but shut it at a wave of the princess' hand.

"And now that I have made all right in your worlds, you argue about where you are to live. I will settle this once and for all. You will exist in both times. I will give you the key to go back and forth between Wulfgar's home and yours."

Wulf opened his mouth to speak, but the princess waved him to silence.

"But you both must stop this badgering and admit you love one another. This was the reason for Wulf being sent forward in time in the first place. He has learned his lesson. Now, little Sparrow, what do you say?"

"It's Raven, not Sparrow, and I say, thank you, Princess."

"Wulfgar?"

"I also offer my thanks, Princess. And if Raven is in agreement, we would be honored to have you at our wedding."

Raven nodded. "Yes, of course. We both would love that."

"Fine, then take this and when you wish to return to either time, all you have to do is place your hand on the key and then think of where you want to be." Catriona's smile slashed white as she held out a golden chain to Wulf. She then did the same to Raven.

"This way, maybe you both won't argue so

much."

Before they could thank her, the princess was gone. The only thing left of her visit was a whisper of sound. "I expect the nuptials to be soon."

****

Raven stood by Wulf's side as they exchanged vows before his people. She accepted the armband that matched his and then the sword he held out to her. She in turn gave him his finger ring as he gave her hers. Together they turned to face the men and women, who raised their voices in a cry of jubilation over their jarl's wedding.

She and Wulf would entertain with a feast before being put to bed in his chamber with orders not to be disturbed until the next evening. Wulf had consented to her request they not have to undress for the bedding ceremony. Their plans were simple: once alone, they both would return to Raven's time for a wedding held in front of her friends and where they could take photos without risking being accused of being in league with the devil.

****

Hours later, Wulf stood with Raven inside her house. The more modern wedding dress she'd exchanged for her medieval finery puddled on the floor by her bed.

"Raven, I know not why I was blessed to find you, but woman if I don't bed you soon, I will die from want."

Raven laughed out loud at the words he had uttered repeatedly from the moment they escaped to the future, during their second wedding, and reception.

"Well, then, what are you waiting for, Viking?"

If was if her words turned a lever on inside Wulf. His eyes became mere slits of silver, and one hand caught her head and then his lips captured hers.

His tongue sought and then forged forward to

seek the warmth inside Raven's mouth. He welcomed her moan of desire and trapped it deep inside his soul. He released her head, ran his hands down the side of her undergarment, and began to unsnap the satin material. Her more than ample breasts fell into his palms. He caressed their fullness, tweaked their hard peaks, and exulted in the fact Raven was his.

He continued his caresses and then released Raven's lips, and bent to take one of the tips into his mouth. His tongue laved and nipped until the nipple stood tall and firm. Raven gripped him at the waist and he caught her hips in his hands, and lifted her so her womanhood pressed against his blood-filled shaft.

"Raven, I need you."

"And I need you."

Wulf pulled her closer and walked backward to the bed. He nibbled a trail of fire down her throat before laying her gently down on the turned down cover.

Raven pulled him closer, not wanting to lose the feel of him against her, yet she wanted to be naked against his body. To feel the hardness of Wulf against her center. To experience that same hardness deep inside her. "You have on too many clothes, Wulf. Take them off."

The swiftness of his response shocked Raven, but only for a moment. She welcomed the brush of his chest against her sensitive breasts, the hardness of his need against her desire-drenched sex. Her hands clenched and then caressed his broad back. Each circuit slid closer to the firm surface of his buttocks.

Wulf's murmurings in his own language teased her ears before his tongue swirled the inner shell and then traced a path to her lips. Once again she was drowning in the heat of his kiss. She loved it, and him. Yet her body yearned for more. She reluctantly left the enticement of his backside and slid her hands between their bodies, where she caressed the hot length of his manhood and with the other hand cupped the firm bag holding his family jewels.

"Raven, you will unman me if you do not stop."

"Just a few minutes longer. I have wanted to touch you for what seems like forever."

His soft laughter turned into a husky groan. "Enough, wife. 'Tis not the time to tease me. I have been full to bursting since I saw you soaking wet in the cemetery and then naked in this very room. I cannot wait any longer."

"Then don't. I'm as anxious as you to make this marriage a real one."

Wulf stepped up his caresses to Raven's breasts as he suckled and nipped his way down her body. A kiss to the inside of both thighs and she whimpered like a puppy. Her cry just made him harder.

He kissed the object of his desire before moving back up her body. This time he wasted no time in touching her soft flesh. He needed to be inside Raven before he lost it like an untried lad.

Wulf nudged her legs open a bit more and then grasped her thighs, pulling her forward until the head of his shaft touched the opening to her drenched channel. He lifted her hips a bit more and then pushed forward. The first grasp of her sex almost had him shooting his lust right then and there. He gritted his teeth. He would not allow himself pleasure until he gave Raven hers.

Raven felt the first touch of his manhood against her feminine opening. A second later, his thumb brushed against the hidden nub nestled just above. Spirals of heat shot through her. A flick, a pinch, a caress, and the bands of desire wove tighter and tighter until she felt as if her body would explode with pleasure. And then it did, rocketing her higher and higher until she fell back to consciousness with

Wulf looking down at her.

"I love you, Raven."

Before she could return her love to him, he pushed forward and took her virginal status with him. A brief flash of pain, and then she experienced what it felt like to make love to a man almost possessed with desire. It took just a moment for her to pick up the rhythm but when she did, Wulf met her even stronger in his thrusts.

Again her body tightened and her hips began to lift off the mattress as she pushed forward seeking the pinnacle of fulfilled desire once again. This time, Wulf's eyes closed as she felt herself falling into the trembling vortex of their combined climaxes.

A while later, she awoke with her head on Wulf's shoulder. The grin he bestowed on her when she dared to look up set up a heat that burned her cheeks.

"I love that you blush, and I love that I be the first man to taste the desire of your body."

Her face heated more, and she could feel the blush cover her breasts as he stared first at her face and then her body.

"You are embarrassing me."

"Why? What we did together was a gift. In all my adulthood I have never felt the way I did when I took what you so freely gave me, Raven."

"Well, I've never felt that way either if it helps. I thought I could imagine what a man and woman felt when I write love scenes in my books, but nothing prepared me for what we did. It'll take me just a bit of time to get used to it."

Wulf tenderly palmed her face with his hand. "Did I hurt you?"

"No, I think you made me so hot that I forgot I'd never been with a man before." She returned his caresses, then moved her hand to slide down the thick column of his throat, and then allowed her palm to rest against his heart.

"I don't know why it took a man from the past to make me believe in love, but I'm truly happy Catriona sent you here."

"Even if her reason for doing so makes me a rutting stag?" His question, although asked with the slightest smile on his lips, seemed to be of the utmost importance to her new husband.

"Well, since that took place in another century, long before I was born, then it is not something we need to worry about. Of course, I expect nothing but faithfulness from you now." Her statement sounded even to her ears as a plea for confirmation he would do just that.

"You never have to fear my straying from your bed. I have all I ever need with you."

Her sign of relief stirred the slight covering of hair on his chest. "Good, now, I guess we should work out some sort of schedule about being here and being in your time. I can't take my computer to your home, it could mess up all types of things for the future."

"What if you write during the day here in your time and then come home to my time for supper?"

Raven sat up in bed. "That could work. As long as we keep your chamber locked, no one should know I'm gone. I'll leave you a message, that way you won't worry."

"Yes, that would be good. And there will be times when the snow is so deep around the longhouse and the village, that no one will venture out. I would welcome the chance to come here with you."

She laughed out loud. "You just don't want to give up a hot shower or the television."

"Yea, you are right. I have grown used to the creature comforts your home offers. I'm also rather fond of what you call fast food."

His nose nuzzled her neck before his lips bit her ear.

"Ouch, what did you do that for?"

"You are too sassy for a new wife."

"Sassy? I'll show you sassy. Fool with me, Viking, and I won't order your favorite pizza for dinner."

"You win, but only because all this time traveling has confused my belly."

"Oh, poor baby." Raven rolled away from Wulf, jumped off the bed, and then headed for the shower.

"Behave or I won't save you any hot water." Her effort to close the door against her fast-moving husband went awry. Instead she found her arms full of aroused Norseman ready to plunder and pillage.

"I believe you need a lesson in how a wife acts. Now, start the water and we will see who cries 'hold' first."

Raven grasped his manhood in her hand and led him toward the shower. "I believe I will just begin like I plan to go on and lead you around by the—"

A light slap to her rear and she let go of his heated flesh. "Don't do that again, Wulf, I'm warning you."

"And what will you do if I do, wife?"

"I'll...think of something, when you least suspect it."

His laughter echoed against the bathroom tile and flung itself back to bathe Raven in its caress. She loved it when he laughed. She loved him.

"Wulf?"

The seriousness of her gaze stopped his laughter.

"What is it, my Raven?"

"You don't think Catriona would ever take back her gift, do you? I mean keep us apart?"

He caught her tense body close to his. "No, I do not think she will do so. I do not know her well, but she seemed to be happy for us at the wedding."

"She was there? I didn't see her."

"All I saw was a mist of colors. I'm surprised she

even came. My intent to let her know when we were to be wed was almost forgotten with all the attention given to us when we returned to my homeland."

"Oh, good. I guess I just wanted to make sure. I never thought I would ever marry, let alone be married to someone like you. I don't want to live in fear that something could go wrong."

"Put your mind at rest. Nothing but death will ever separate us. Now, get in that shower. I want to see if I can make you moan while under the water."

Raven did as he asked, and it wasn't until much, much later they sat at the table gorging on pizza. "So you're okay with not being at your home all the time?"

"Yes, wife, let me assure you again. Whether we be here or in the past, it does not matter. For wherever you are is where I'll be home."

"**Derek, I assume there's a reason you** ruined my song, and treated me like you were from the caveman era."

"Why? You have to ask why?" Derek glared down at her. What was his problem?

"Are you dense as well as rude?" Cat slung back at him.

"Lady, you were this close to being booed off the stage for sounding like a scalded cat. Then you start acting like a stripper with an itch to scratch. This is a family restaurant. You can't act that way in public." The last of his tirade came out on a sigh. Cat looked, really looked, at his face. The lines around his eyes were deeper; he looked like he didn't sleep enough.

Instead of the tongue-lashing she wanted to give him, she found herself reaching up and touching his face. "You need more sleep."

As she watched, his green eyes turned darker. His previously stiff lips thinned into somewhat of a smile.

"Princess, you pull out all the stops." He slid his arm around her and sat her on the back of the car. She liked it. This way she could look in his face without craning her neck.

"In what way?" She asked her question, curious as to what he meant by stops.

"You blow hot and then cold and then you look like a spitting cat and turn into a kitten who needs to be petted." Derek just stared at her while she tried to figure out his words. For some reason she didn't think he meant them derogatively. It seemed he was as confused by her as she was by him. Maybe her first estimate that he was just a snobby mortal was off base.

"I wouldn't mind being petted by you."

Semper Fi Magick

by

Faith V. Smith

Dedication

As always, to my darling angel Rick!
You are missed and loved.
And to my precious daughter, Amanda,
thank you for always being the best support
a mom and author could have. Love you!
To God be the glory,
and to all our heroes in arms, may God bless you
and keep you out of harm's way.
Thank you for protecting us and keeping us safe.
And to Sarah Hansen, editor extraordinaire,
thank you for loving my books!

A fine line separates the mortal world from the faery realm. To traverse the strand and interact with mortals can and does cost penalties from the Seelie Court to those who tread where they should not when it comes to matters of the heart.

Chapter One

Catriona, princess, and daughter of King Tiernan and the deceased Alisanne, passed the emery board across her bright red nails. Faery dust, she was bored wingless. After her last sojourn into the mortal realm, the king of the Tuatha De Danann restricted her interference in business not her own. Dear old Da, the man most of the time didn't act like she existed, but let her do something (that, in her opinion, was wonderful) and he threatened to pull her wings.

For the last six moon cycles, she'd hosted parties, helped to mediate problems in the faery realm, and now wanted to pull her hair out. She missed the interplay with mortals. They were boring at times, endearing on occasion, but always comical in their reactions to love.

The emery board hit the top of her bedside table, and Catriona threw herself back against the mounds of pillows on her bed. The gauzy purple, blue, and green bed curtains drew her eye for a moment. Maybe she should do some redecorating. It would serve her da right. He hated when things were in chaos. She could redo the entire palace.

No, he'd just look at her and shake his head. His bright green eyes would look sad, and then she'd feel lower than an asp.

Two silver moons shone in through the turret window, casting a soft glow throughout the room. It reminded her of Wulfgar Thorrason's eyes. Now that was a mortal she enjoyed tampering with. He and his new bride were the products of her interference. It would serve her da right if she disappeared for a bit. Yes, she would be breaking his law, but the man needed to treat her like a daughter and not so much a princess. It would be nice if he trusted her judgment, which for the most part was pretty damn good.

She picked up a golden pitcher, engraved with flowers and leaves, and poured herself a good helping of ambrosia. It wasn't as strong as some of the mortal drinks she'd sampled, but it would do—for now anyway.

****

Seven days later, Catriona hugged her father goodbye. He was headed to the outer reaches of the kingdom on business. Just the chance she'd been waiting for. She could pop into the mortal realm and pop back without anyone being the wiser. Celine, her sister, whose niece had ended up in Wulfgar's bed (without any repercussions, thank the faeries) was leaving today and taking the little hussy with her. After talking to her niece she felt badly she'd zapped Wulfgar into the future without asking his side of the story. Any who, it had all worked out.

She flashed back to her chamber, waved her hand, and then prepared to zap herself to Wulfgar and Raven's home.

****

Derek knocked back another cold beer and let the conversation between his cousin Rav and her new husband filter around him. God in Heaven, he was tired. Not just in body but in mind. As a Special Ops Marine, he was used to missions being dangerous, but the last one had almost been deadly for everyone in his unit. The nightmares left over from that experience was one of the reasons he was on R&R. His commander thought he needed to come to grips with his guilt. A guilt the Marine Corps thought was misplaced.

He wasn't sure if they were right or not. It didn't matter either way. Derek would never forget the blood or the wounded and dying.

"Hey Derek, you have to stop thinking so much. You know what your commander said."

Raven's copper-colored hair bounced on her shoulders as she tossed a paperback at him. His cousin, a romance author, seemed to have found her own true-life love story. He was happy for her and Wulfgar (strange name for a man) seemed like a nice enough guy. A bit old-fashioned at times, but he'd been the perfect host since Derek had kinda just dropped in on them.

"I know, cuz, but give me a break. It's hard to stop thinking completely." Derek tempered the snarling rage that lately seemed to ride just beneath the surface of his skin.

Raven slid out of her new husband's embrace, and moved to sit next to Derek on the sofa. "Honey, you did all you could. You have to realize that and try to move on."

He patted the hand she laid on his chest, but couldn't force a smile to his lips. Raven had always been the dreamer in the family. She looked for good in others and tried to make things right. He loved her dearly, but sometimes he just needed to be left alone. Maybe coming here was a bad idea, but he couldn't face his quarters on base. The memories seemed so much stronger there, so he'd caught a lift on a transport plane to spend his four weeks off duty with family.

"I know, baby, and I appreciate you trying to help." He dropped a kiss on her hand and then rolled off the couch. "If you guys don't mind, I think I'm gonna go for a walk. I'll be back for dinner."

****

Catriona enjoyed the open-mouthed stares of Wulfgar and Raven when she popped in.

"Catriona, what a surprise." Raven recovered before Wulfgar, and the smile she sent Catriona was warm if a bit weak. Wulf however scowled like he smelled bad meat.

"What do we owe this visit to, Princess?"

"Please...Wulfgar...you act like I'm your enemy. I thought all that was behind you. After all, you did find your soul mate, you have the best of both worlds, and if I'm not mistaken you seem to be really happy."

The growl he tossed her way was bereft of any rage. Yes, he knew who his faery godmother, or better yet, make that *sister,* was.

"So, do you care if I stay for a while? "

Raven, brave mortal, took Catriona by the hand and led her into the kitchen.

"Have a seat, Cat, I hope you don't mind if I call you that. It seems to me, you are here for something other than butting in, right?"

Cat allowed her lips to curl up. Raven hit the wand right on its tip. "You're right. And yes, Cat's fine. I'm bored senseless, and wanted to visit people who did not have wings or the attention span for only faery issues." Cat flicked a strand of hair out of her eyes.

Raven poured something into a glass container, added a bit of something else and then the container made a whirring sound. A moment later, she placed a tall glass with salt around the rim and a lime slice in front of Cat.

"Drink up, Princess. I think I know exactly what's wrong with you."

"God help us all!" Wulfgar's groan echoed throughout the room.

"Wulf, that was totally uncalled for. You have no

idea what I have planned."

Wulf moved behind Raven and locked his arms around her waist. Cat envied the tenderness he conveyed when he pulled her back against him.

"You forget, wife. I know you. Your life revolves around making romance in books. I've seen that particular gleam in your eyes before—right before you threw some poor man into the arms of a woman in one of your pages of work."

The giggle coming from Raven should have made Cat cringe, but instead, she wondered what it felt like to have someone love her for just being her. It certainly would be a novelty. Since infancy, faery males had thrown themselves, at first at her father and then at her, in an effort to gain an alliance with the king. She didn't want that type of relationship. She wanted something like the couple in front of her had—love that would survive no matter what circumstances.

"I'm all wings. Tell me what you have in mind, Raven." Cat took a sip of the icy drink in front of her and then licked her lips. "What is this? It's wonderful, better than ambrosia."

"It's called a margarita. I love them. They're inspirational for a night of writing."

Cat wondered what else the salty, tart drink could inspire.

"First, I think we need to make you look less like a princess, and more like the girl next door."

****

A short time later, Cat admired herself in the full-length mirror. The jeans most mortals seemed so fond of hugged her thighs and hips. The T-shirt, as Raven called it, was a bright purple and did amazing things to her upper chest. Cat took the jewelry Raven offered and attached the round and quite large hoops to her earlobes.

"You know, I could really hate you."

"Why?" Catriona's confusion was genuine. Raven's lips and eyes smiled but her words were the direct opposite.

"Because you look awesome without any makeup at all. If I tried that, I'd look like an old shoe."

Cat smiled. It felt strange to get a compliment from someone who didn't want something in return.

"Thank you, Raven. I am a bit off my world so to speak. I've never had a friend before."

"Oh, honey, don't you worry about anything. I'll be your friend." Raven's hug made Cat feel like she actually belonged. That she was a person and not just a princess.

"Thank you. I wonder what Wulfgar will say." She had to admit, his reaction so far had not been what she'd hoped. He acted like she'd intruded. Well, she had, but it wasn't meant to cause harm.

"Don't worry about my husband. He'll get over it. Besides, I think you'll be just the thing to get my cousin out of his guilt trip."

"Cousin?"

"Yes, Derek. He's had a hard time of it lately."

She wasn't sure if she wanted to be the balm to raise someone's mood, but—

A door slammed somewhere in the house. "Hey, Rav, I'm back."

"Oh good, he's home. Come on."

For the first time since she embarked on her little defiance adventure, Cat wondered if she should have stayed in the faery realm.

****

Derek held his breath as his greeting to Rav hit the air. He hoped she'd gone on one of the little disappearing trips she and her new husband were so fond of. When asked where they got off to, both were closed-mouthed. Of course, they could be exercising their newlywed status. If he remembered correctly, one year signified the end of being goofy and rutting like rabbits. Of course, he'd never been married. Lisa, his ex-fiancée, blew that dream apart when she slept with one of his now ex-best friends.

He snagged a beer from the fridge, and popped the top as he went around the corner to the living room. The can was at his lips when a movement out of the corner of his eye caused him to stop as quickly as a deer caught in headlights.

She wouldn't. Would she? Yeah, knowing his cousin she wanted to stick everyone with a happy-ever-after like in her romance books—only it wasn't gonna work with him. No way would he allow the petite blue-eyed blond in tight-fitting jeans and a top that showed almost to a shadow what nature had given her to affect him. Not even if she got on her knees and promised him the best time of his life, it wasn't gonna happen.

"Derek, I'm so glad you're back."

"I just bet you are." His words were a snarl, but he didn't care.

"Derek! There's no need to take that tone with me." Raven's voice held tears. He wanted to tell her he was sorry but before he could, she tugged the woman forward—presenting her almost like a gift.

"I want you to meet Prin—I mean Cat, short for Catriona. She's going to be visiting for a bit, too."

Rude it might be, but he didn't try to suppress the groan escaping his lips. The look Raven leveled his way was paired with an equally stern look at Wulf who entered the room just in time to hear the bombshell.

With no way out, he'd have to play nice for the moment, but he certainly didn't need a woman that reminded him of Lisa, his ex.

"Hi, nice to meet you."

The smile she gave him was high-voltage. Another reason to get the hell out of Dodge.

"It's nice to meet you too." She held her hand out, and he wondered what the heck he was supposed to do with it.

After a moment, she pulled it back and the sparkle in her eye turned a shade darker. It looked like he might have pissed the woman off.

Maybe he should try to make amends. If she was going to be staying here also, he didn't need female hysterics to dampen the rest of his leave.

"Look, I'm sorry, Catri—"

"That's Princess Catriona to you."

Was the woman for real? She sounded serious. What a stuck-up witch. No way would he call her a princess.

"Not in this day and age, sweetheart. You might look like a wet dream but you aren't royalty."

The hiss she sent his way coincided with gasps from both Raven and Wulf. What on earth was the matter with them? All three of them.

****

Cat drew back her hand to deliver a ball of fire right at the pompous ass masquerading as Raven's cousin. There was no way the rude, although so handsome man, could be kin to the sweet, kind woman holding onto her arm. She bestowed a smile on Raven, and then felt her eyes go dark with the beginning of her magick.

Chapter Two

"Please, Cat, don't do it. Derek's really a good guy, he's just had a bad time with women." Raven's plea caught her attention. What kind of bad time could the mortal have? He didn't look like anything troubled him. In fact he looked quite fine to Catriona.

His eyes were a reflection of green much like the forests surrounding the castle. His brows were arches of ripe wheat, as was the color of the hair resting just above his jacket. He was quite a handsome fellow, but his manners were that of a peasant. "For you, I'll leave him alone—for now. Rude as he is, I am a guest here and will try not to make any trouble."

Raven and Wulfgar's sighs were loud in the now silent room. She waited to see if the other mortal would speak.

"What's wrong with you people? You act like she's a frigging goddess or something."

Cat felt the leash she had on her temper loosen. How dare he compare her to a goddess? Most goddesses were promiscuous, not to mention they drank to excess, and were always ready to hurl lightning bolts at any hapless faery in their line of sight.

"Princess, she is a princess. For God's sake, don't get her upset." Wulf's statement and exclamation was met with a grin from their rude guest.

"For real? She's really a princess?"

"Yes." Raven's affirmation was whispered.

"Of what? Pampered rich girls?"

Cat lobbed the fireball she'd hidden behind her back straight at the mortal. His eyes went wide, his mouth opened, but he managed to jump out of the way, still holding onto the can in his hand. She needed to practice her throwing methods.

"What the hell was that?" Instead of waiting for her to answer, he set the metal container down, tugged off his jacket and began to beat out the slight fire eating the bookcase next to him. Once finished, he stalked, for that was the only way she could describe his walk, to her. "Lady, are you crazy? What type of device did you use to start that fire, and why on Earth did you try to kill me?"

His voice, raised in anger, still sounded like a husky and sensual caress to Cat's ears.

"If you mean my mind is not right, then you are wrong. I am perfectly fine mentally. And I did not try to kill you." At his raised brow she spat, "If I had wanted to, then you would be dead."

The expression on his face didn't really make her happy. For some reason, he looked like a cross between a cornered animal and a man who was at the end of his patience.

"Raven, can you explain what your more-than-a-bit-nuts houseguest means?"

Catriona shook off Raven's arm. "I need no one to explain for me. I am Catriona, Princess of the Tu Danuan."

"You are more than crazy, woman." Derek turned his gaze to Raven. "Look, I think the best thing for me to do is pack and leave. I appreciate you letting me stay here, but four's a bit crowded." He glanced back at Cat. "If you know what I mean."

For some reason, as angry as he made her, she didn't want him to leave. She also didn't like the almost tearful look on Raven's face, not to mention the glowering gaze Wulf was bestowing on her and Derek. Maybe she could make amends? Besides, something about Derek drew her to him, like the stars drawing power from the moon.

"I apologize. There is no need for you to leave, Derek. My behavior was atrocious, not at all becoming of a princess."

She waited to see if he would accept her apology and give her one in return. He did neither, just a quick shrug of his shoulders, and he headed back the way he came.

Cat started to follow him.

"Cat, maybe you should let him cool off a bit. I'll tell him it was just a magick trick. Now, let's go for a walk, and I'll fill you in on why Derek's being such an ass."

Curiosity won out over wanting to lob another fireball at the man.

"All right. I'll go with you."

Cat scooted past Wulf, who quit glaring long enough to place a kiss on Raven's lips, and then they were out the door.

The spring weather lifted her spirits, but only a bit. Try as she might, she couldn't reason why she was drawn to the over-grown oaf who'd insulted her. Men fawned over her. Derek—she allowed his name to tease her mind—was the opposite. He acted as if she was some type of abomination. Not to mention, he thought she was deranged.

"Let's stop here." Raven's voice broke into her thoughts. So busy with the problem of Derek, she almost ran into the bench her new friend gestured toward.

Catriona sat down and gave herself marks for not wiping it off first. She was in the mortal realm, and a bit of dust and something she didn't want to think about on the iron seat wouldn't hurt her.

"Cat, I want to tell you a story."

"About Derek?" She couldn't quite contain her excitement.

Raven's eyes lit with laughter for the space of a second before her blue gaze dimmed.

"Yes. Derek is a bit jaded. He's a good guy, he really is. A fine Marine, but he's hurting right now for a couple of reasons. He found his fiancée in bed with another man. A really good friend of his. He was just getting his head back together when he got called up on a mission."

Fiancée? No wonder the man was down on women. Maybe she could change his mind. Of course, she'd have to change her attitude also. It wouldn't do to come on as Princess Witch with a capital *B* if she wanted to get closer to him. And she definitely wanted to obtain that goal.

"...he lost one of his men during the attack. Now he blames himself."

Attack? She must have missed something. Cat tilted her head and concentrated on Raven. The words she'd just spoken came back to her. Pinned down, under enemy fire. From what she'd read of this century, she ascertained it was a military operation.

"Was Derek hurt?"

"No thank God, but the inner guilt is eating him alive." Raven caught and held Cat's hand. "I know you'll be good for him, but you can't try to kill him again, Cat."

"I know, and I'm sorry I tried to hit him in the first place. I truly would not have killed him, Raven. It would be rude to do that in your home."

Raven's eyes went wide.

"Not that I would have killed him elsewhere. I just meant I was angry, and I forgot to control my magick."

"Whew, you scared me for a minute. Now, do you understand why Derek can be a bit..."

12

"Rude? I do, but I don't like it. I mean, he acted like I was a piece of ruined fruit." Cat stuck her nose in the air to emphasize her point.

"Well, if you can ignore him, all the better."

Catriona wasn't sure if she could ignore the mortal. Not one soul, immortal or otherwise, had fascinated her as much as this man. She would, however, be on her best behavior.

****

Derek followed Wulf out onto the patio. He needed the air. From the first moment he laid eyes on Cat, or was it Catriona, he hadn't been able to think of anything else. He knew better, but he couldn't help himself. The woman spoke to him on a baser level, igniting lust and a bit of something he didn't want to think about. Lust was okay, he enjoyed having a woman in his bed. Not often and definitely not since Lisa. He'd learned that lesson, and didn't plan on going back to school any time soon.

The something else, however, bugged the hell out of him. He'd met Lisa right when he graduated from college and right before he enlisted in the Corps sometime after the first Iraqi war. She'd seemed enthralled with the idea her boyfriend was going to be a Marine. Told all her girlfriends and family she would eventually be a military wife, but then she became disenchanted with his job and him.

Derek could still hear her voice the afternoon of their last meeting.

"I don't see why we can't go out. You never want to do anything when you're on leave." Her sexy pout didn't win her any points. He was tired of battling her over his job.

"I'm tired. I told you that when I called home before going R&R." Derek flopped down on the couch in his apartment. He'd only been home an hour when Lisa showed up. He was glad to see her, of course he was, for all of the one minute it took for her to start bitching at him.

"Use English please. Not all of us are in the military." Her words, uttered from sensually colored lips, caused his blood pressure to go up.

"Get used to it, babe. You'll have to adapt when we get married."

Her huff of air he ignored. He even tried to ignore the wheedling, pleading attempts on her part to change his mind that day. What he couldn't let go was the nasty word she hurled at the Marine Corps in general.

"I think you need to go home, Lisa."

"If I do, I may not come back." The statement was a taunt to get some kind of reaction out of him. Although, it wasn't the one she evidently wanted.

"Suit yourself."

Derek heard the rattle of ice and then caught the can Wulf tossed his way, popped the top, and drained half its contents.

"Thanks."

"You are welcome." His cousin-in-law didn't say anything else just took a seat on one of the deck chairs.

Derek went back to his thoughts. After about thirty minutes, he'd cooled off and decided to go to Lisa's place to apologize. He used the key she'd given him months before and let himself in. Her car was in the driveway so he knew she was home. The radio was playing in the bedroom, and he thought she might be getting ready for a bath. Lisa liked music, candles, and a glass of wine when she bathed. She also loved making love in the garden tub in her bathroom.

He slid his shoes off, crept up to the slightly ajar door, and then pushed it open. The grin on his face turned to dust. Lisa was in the bath, but not alone. His good friend Sgt. Casey Mallory was sucking tongue with his fiancée while fondling her more-than-adequate boobs. He didn't have to see beneath the bubbles to know they were attached like a couple of dogs in heat.

Without saying a word, he'd walked out, leaving his shoes, and any other articles of clothing he'd left at her place since they became serious. Not since that night four months ago had he laid eyes on Lisa.

Of course, it wasn't Cat's fault her coloring reminded him of the treacherous bitch. In all fairness, he should have handled the situation better. But the woman actually got under his skin, not to mention waking up his sex-drive. A drive that had been all but dead since Lisa.

"I am not that good with English, but if you need to vent, as Raven calls it, I will be happy to listen." Wulf's words pulled him back to the present.

"Women, you can't live with 'em, you can't—"

"Derek, don't you dare finish that sentence. And I thank you to keep your views to yourself. Wulf comes from a long line of warr—men who think women have to be protected. He's bad enough as it is."

His cheeks heated a bit. Raven had snuck up on him, something that would get him killed while on a mission. Maybe he needed to see if he could score some more R&R.

"Sorry, cuz." He looked around but didn't see the other houseguest.

"Cat's changing clothes, she'll be right out."

This time the heat went up a notch in his face. He hoped no one else noticed.

"I thought we'd go out to dinner if that's okay with you guys." Raven slid into Wulf's embrace as Derek watched. The couple made hearts and roses seem possible, but he knew better.

"Fine with me, what about you, Wulf?"

The look the man shot his wife looked like a

mixture of adoration and excitement to Derek.

"Can we go to the steak house?"

"Sure, darling. We'll leave as soon as Cat's ready."

His host's face fell for just a moment. "I did not think Catriona would be going with us."

Raven pulled away from Wulf, gave him a glare, and followed it up with one in Derek's direction. "Look, you two, Cat's a good person. Wulf, you know if it wasn't for her, we never would have met. And Derek, you've already been more than rude to her. Try using some of that Marine charm."

He opened his mouth to protest—

"I mean it! I want this to be a happy evening for all of us."

The door to the deck opened. "Now behave!" Raven's warning was barely a whisper, but both the men got the message.

"Hi, sorry to make you wait on me."

Despite his determination to do nothing more than to say a quick "That's okay," Derek found himself staring at Catriona, who looked like a succulent steak on a plate to a starving man. Gone were the form-fitting jeans and T-shirt. The sweeping gown swayed in the late afternoon breeze, teasing him as it touched and then flowed away from her curved hips. Highlighting legs that would be just the right length to toss over his shoulder as he plumbed the depths of her feminine and hot-as-hell body.

The deep neckline caressed mounds of flesh his hands hungered to touch, and his mouth craved to taste.

"Derek?"

Raven's amused tone pulled him free of the flesh-burning thoughts overriding his common sense.

"Yeah?" He took a sip of his beer.

"You okay with steak and baked potatoes?"

The liquid drained down his windpipe, Derek started coughing, and then groaned when Wulf slapped him on the back.

"Steak is fine." The S-word almost caused him to strangle again. He needed to get a hold of his lust. Lust he didn't need.

"Great, so let's go."

Raven grabbed Wulf's arm, directed a pointed stare toward Cat, and then waited for him to offer his arm.

"Thank you." Cat's sultry tone did nothing to tamp down his desire. Lord, how on Earth would he get through dinner?

"I'm truly sorry about what happened before." The apology was unexpected, and it made him feel like a cad for causing the problem in the first place.

"It's okay, it wasn't really your fault. I overreacted."

The slight hold Cat had on his arm was doing strange things to his body and his psyche. Maybe he should just hightail it out tomorrow. Yeah, he hated to be a coward, but the woman was beginning to scare the hell out of him. He never wanted to put himself in a position where he couldn't trust the woman he loved ever again. If he made the mistake of falling for Ms. Sexy Thing, then he'd never know if she was faithful or not while on maneuvers. Women like Cat drew men like a thunderstorm drew lightning.

"Well, let's put all that behind us." Cat's words reminded him they were at the car and he should play gentleman by opening the door. He did and she just stood there.

"Aren't you going to get in?" His question hung in the air until Wulf fielded it.

"Princess, it is all right. A method of travel."

"Oh, thank you, Wulf." Although the explanation

seemed strange to Derek, it seemed to help Cat. She scooted onto the backseat, and he followed. Raven sat behind the wheel. Her husband must have a lot of faith in her. A lot of men he knew would not be comfortable with a woman driving, especially when they were not alone. It didn't bother him, and maybe Wulf was so much in love, he didn't care either.

Cat oohed and ahhed out the window for about five minutes before she leaned back against the seat. She acted like she'd never seen anything like the small town his cousin lived in. In fact, she seemed unfamiliar with a lot of things come to think of it. Where was the woman from? Some backwater town or a nunnery?

Naw, she'd never survive in a nunnery. Too much life dancing in the blue of her eyes.

The ride to the restaurant consisted of mostly silence on the part of all the vehicle's occupants. Catriona stared out the window and made several more little oohing sounds, but no one addressed them. Strange how everything, from a pedestrian in bright colors to the cars flying by, seemed to delight her.

While Cat watched the world, he watched Cat. The woman was either a very good actress for showing innocence and guile, or she really was fresh as a babe in the woods.

Upon arriving and after being seated at the steak house, Derek still could not pull his gaze from the sensual Catriona. A circumstance that seemed to amuse his cousin and her husband who exchanged smiles.

"Are you ready to order now, Derek?"

He turned back and felt the heat hit his face when he realized their waitress stood there with her pen and pad.

"Sorry, give me just a second." A quick flip to open the menu, and he ordered the first entree he saw.

"Uh, not sure you really want to order that, hon."

"What do you mean?"

"Well, you just ordered shellfish, and you're allergic to it."

If the heat in his face was an indicator, it and the rest of his body was a bright red.

"Yeah, you're right. I must have misread it."

Raven chuckled, took the menu from his hand, and handed it to the waitress. "Bring him a sirloin steak, medium rare, with a salad and baked potato. House dressing. Oh, and a nice cold beer."

Derek wanted to crawl under the table, and did duck his head for a moment, studying the place setting in front of him. A moment later, he braved a glance around the table. Raven and Wulf were staring at one another with that infernal lovesick look, whereas Catriona was busy studying the restaurant.

He should really say something, but what? Before he could decide on a topic, the woman turned to him.

"So, did you want to kill your ex-fiancée?"

Chapter Three

Her question blew him away. Raven had been ultra busy in dispersing his business. He'd have a talk with her after dinner. Right now, how to answer the woman giving him a sympathetic look.

"Well, at that moment, I did, but I thought better of it."

"Why? If you were bonded to her, then she should not have abused you." Catriona looked about as confused as Derek felt.

"Do you mean engaged?"

She worried her lip with her teeth before responding. "Yes, I think that's the word Raven used."

"Murder can get you life in prison or the death penalty. Lisa wasn't worth it."

"I don't understand. Why would someone kill you for something like that? It would be justified."

Derek wished the princess would let it go. He looked around, and was saved by the waitress bearing food. His sigh of relief was heartfelt.

His tablemate thanked the waitress and then speared a bite of lettuce with her fork. Her movements were dainty, almost hypnotic. Derek grabbed his own cutlery and did some serious damage to his salad. For some reason his appetite was back. He wondered if it had anything to do with meeting Ms. Princess. A woman that could make him forget all rationale if he let her. It was for that reason once every bite of food was gone he decided to chat up Wulf. About time he got to know the man

Raven had chosen.

"So Wulf, what is it you said you did for a living?"

"He's in weaponry."

"I am a jarl."

Neither Raven's nor Wulf's explanation made sense, still he'd bite. "So what type of weaponry, and jarl of what?"

Raven's eyes went wide. If he didn't know better, he'd think she was a bit panicked. Her husband however looked like he was really going to warm up to the topic. That would be a change; so far Wulf had pretty much kept quiet when Derek was around.

"I run my family's estate. Take care of the people depending on me to protect them."

Whoa, he sounded like an archaic throwback, but he'd ask anyway. It beat engaging Catriona in conversation. A sideways glance showed the princess delicately licking her lips. Damn, that move should be outlawed in public. Derek fought the lust filling his rod. He swallowed to clear the lump in his throat.

"What do they need protecting from?"

"Raiders."

"What?" Surely he'd misheard the guy. There weren't any raiders in this part of Michigan or the States either for that matter.

Raven frantically waved at their waitress who promptly came over.

"Derek, why don't you have another beer. I think I want something a bit stronger while we wait on our steaks."

His cousin looked frazzled as she ordered two margaritas, he assumed one was for Cat, or he hoped it was, and two more beers for him and Wulf.

"So what about these—" Derek froze as Catriona's hand bumped his thigh.

Faith V. Smith

He jerked so hard he almost tilted his chair backward. And the fact Cat tried to help him only made matters worse. Her hand landed right on the hardness pressing against the front of his zipper.

The princess's eyes grew large, and her hand snapped back, right before his beer went flying into his lap. Not how he'd like to cool off, but the ice-cold brew did the trick.

"Oh no, I'm so sorry!" She grabbed her napkin and began to dab the wet spot. Derek saw lust-filled stars. His grip wasn't all that gentle when he caught the delicate weapon.

"It's okay, I'm fine. I don't need your help." The last part came out in a harsh tone, and Cat looked a bit hurt. Damn, he couldn't have that.

"Look, it's really okay." He gave her a smile that probably resembled the worse grimace in the world due to his extreme discomfort. He ignored the looks Raven and Wulf sent his way but could have shouted halleluiah when the waitress brought their food and newly ordered drinks.

Catriona's gaze gleamed with something but what he wasn't sure of before she thanked the waitress who placed a giant-size steak in front of her. If she ate all of that, he'd be surprised, but then again, the woman had been full of surprises since the moment they first met.

Derek ignored his damp jeans and ardor. At least he could eat now without being afraid his lust would get completely out of control.

****

Once the plates were cleared and another round of drinks ordered, Catriona finally achieved a tenth of the dignity she lost after trying to pat Derek's jeans dry. Lord, she didn't have to be a mage to know what the hardness under the napkin was. While she could still hide under a magical stone with embarrassment, she couldn't help but feel curious

22

about what Derek would feel like without his jeans. What would he look like? Did she even care? The man acted like she'd attacked him. It was an accident. Fine, if he wanted to act all male, she didn't care—not one bit.

She purposely avoided looking at the mortal, took a sip of her drink, and then watched as a young man walked to a small, upraised platform. He took a microphone, if she remembered correctly from her research on modern things, and began to sing. The tune wasn't a bad one, and he actually sounded good. The crowd clapped, and he launched into a second song. As he sung about somebody's broken heart, Cat glanced sideways at Derek. Even his gaze was glued to the platform.

Maybe that would be a way to get his attention. It didn't look all that hard. When the man exited the platform, she made her move. She heard gasps from her table as she walked up the steps. She picked up the microphone, looked over several titles of songs, and finally settled on a love ballad. Cat punched the number, watched the lyrics jump up on a tiny screen, and began to sing. A few seconds into the song she heard something like a hiss, quickly followed by someone yelling, "Boo." She assumed it was some type of cheering that mortals did, although she didn't hear it when the previous song was sung.

She decided to give them a performance they would never forget and began to twist and shimmy to the music. The hisses and boos stopped immediately, and Cat wasn't sure if that was a good thing or not. Before she could decide, a pair of arms snaked around her waist, the microphone dropped and made an ear-splitting squeal, and she found herself looking at the floor as someone tossed her over their shoulder.

This time there were shouts. "Put the little lady back down! We were enjoying the show." But whoever had her didn't stop; he just kept right on walking—through the restaurant, out the front door to the car. Once there he thunked her on her feet. She peered up at him, all the time trying to keep from toppling over. She did not care for the dizziness attacking her head or for macho men. "Derek, I assume there's a reason you ruined my song, and treated me like you were from the caveman era."

"Why? You have to ask why?" Derek glared down at her. What was his problem?

"Are you dense as well as rude?" Cat slung back at him.

"Lady, you were this close to being booed off the stage for sounding like a scalded cat. Then you start acting like a stripper with an itch to scratch. This is a family restaurant. You can't act that way in public." The last of his tirade came out on a sigh. Cat looked, really looked, at his face. The lines around his eyes were deeper; he looked like he didn't sleep enough.

Instead of the tongue-lashing she wanted to give him, she found herself reaching up and touching his face. "You need more sleep."

As she watched, his green eyes turned darker. His previously stiff lips thinned into somewhat of a smile.

"Princess, you pull out all the stops." He slid his arm around her and sat her on the back of the car. She liked it. This way she could look in his face without craning her neck.

"In what way?" She asked her question, curious as to what he meant by stops.

"You blow hot and then cold and then you look like a spitting cat and turn into a kitten who needs to be petted." Derek just stared at her while she tried to figure out his words. For some reason she didn't think he meant them derogatively. It seemed he was as confused by her as she was by him. Maybe her first estimate that he was just a snobby mortal was off base.

"I wouldn't mind being petted by you." The moment the words left her mouth she clapped her hand over her lips. She had not planned on voicing the thought that popped into her head. However, she couldn't turn away from the intense look in his eyes, almost as if he were eyeing a piece of candy to devour.

"And I might not mind petting you, but we need to get a few things straight." Derek backed away just a bit.

"One, you have to stop acting like a princess. It's irritating when you do the I'm-better-than-you act." He held up his finger as she started to speak.

"I'm not finished. Two, you have to start acting more like Raven. Don't be putting your stuff out there in public. Someone could get the wrong idea. Three, cut a guy some slack. We like to make the first move." After he spoke his piece, Derek watched to see what Cat would do. He figured she'd either start crying or yelling. He hoped it was neither.

"I can't stop acting like a princess. I am one. I will try not to put my stuff out there, whatever that means, in public, and why is it women have to wait here in the mortal realm? We don't do that where I come from." Catriona's words were softly spoken, and surprised the hell out of him. She didn't seem angry, just perplexed, which made two of them. Why was she going off on mortal realms?

"Okay, fine, but I don't want to hear you're a princess a hundred times a day while I'm here. All right?"

At her nod, he felt himself began to mellow. Okay, she was hot, and agreeing with him made him want to kiss her so why was he just standing there? He moved closer, eased his arms around her slim waist, ducked his head, and captured her lips. His first taste was of lime and salt, but as he coaxed her mouth to open for him, he tasted a blend of exotic spices—ambrosia, cinnamon, cloves. Where the intoxicating trio came from he had no idea, but he loved how she tasted. He deepened his kiss and would have pushed her back on the hood to explore more, but a hard grip on his arm got his attention. He released Cat's lips, touched her face lightly, and turned to face an open-mouthed Raven and a furious Wulf.

Chapter Four

"Man, have you no shame? You can't maul a woman on the street, especially not Catriona. Do you want to get us all speared by lightning bolts?" The man's words hit Derek where it hurt—his sense of honor. Although the reference to lightning bolts seemed a bit severe.

"You're right. I'm sorry. I just..." Nothing he could say would make it better. He averted his gaze from Raven's and Wulf's as he helped Cat off the car. Silence reigned as they all got in the vehicle and continued on the drive back to the house. His host still looked angrier than a kicked anthill. Catriona wouldn't look at him at all; her delicate face stained a beautiful shade of pink, and in the rearview mirror, Raven just looked worried as she drove right at the speed limit.

Something wasn't right; it couldn't be just the kiss. Raven and Wulf kissed all the time and more. Yeah they were married, but his cousin had never been a prude, she'd had her share of lip-locks before she married Thorasson. So why the disturbed attitude? And it wasn't like Cat hadn't enjoyed the kiss too. He might have been out of the loop for a while but that didn't mean he didn't know when a woman was involved physically.

When they arrived back at the house, Wulf exited the car first. After turning off the engine, Raven gave Derek a slight smile before following her husband into the house—leaving him and Cat alone.

"Look, I don't normally come on all macho, but

it's not like you pushed me away. I don't know what Wulf's problem is, but I'm not going to apologize for the kiss, although the timing could have been better."

Cat finally turned her head and gave him a look. "Then don't. I didn't complain did I?"

Her question threw him for a loop. He would have thought she'd be the one up in arms. "Okay, well then, I guess we should go in the house." Derek opened his door, walked around, and did the same for Cat. The sensual grace in which she exited the car did all kinds of things to his male libido. She could make mincemeat out of a man without even trying.

He took her arm, like a gentleman should, and escorted her into the house. Loud voices greeted their entrance.

"How can you say that, Raven? Your kin crossed the line. She is a princess, for God's sake. Men have been drawn and quartered for looking at women like her." Wulf's baritone sounded like he was still pissed. And what on Earth did he mean by drawn and quartered? The man acted like he lived in the Middle Ages, or even earlier. Time to put a stop to this.

"Wulf, please calm down. This is not the time to get so worked up. I want you to go back to the longhouse, work out with your men, cleave someone in half if you have to, but when you come back here, you better behave." Raven's tone, which had started out as just upset, now sounded as angry as her husband's. And Derek was still shooting in the dark. Something was off with the married couple. Not to mention Cat, who was standing stock-still and white as a ghost. He started to tell her it would be okay, but she squared her shoulders, her eyes went all fiery, and she pushed past him into the living room.

"Enough! I don't owe you an explanation,

Wulfgar, but I'm offering you one even if you two are fighting over something that is not your business." Catriona walked right up to the disgruntled Wulf.

"Now, get this straight. Derek did not just kiss me, I kissed him back. I wanted to, and if I want to go to bed with him, then that's my business also."

Before he could pull his mind back from the tantalizing idea of bedding Cat, she just disappeared in a blur of colors. No, that couldn't be right. Something had to be wrong with his eyes. He shut them, reopened them, and found that Catriona indeed was no longer in the room.

"What in the hell just happened?" Derek's voice exploded in a roar causing Wulf to turn to him and Raven to jump.

"'Tis none of your business, cousin." The older man fairly spit out his words, causing a blaze of temper to flare in Derek. He crossed the room and stood toe-to-toe with his cousin's husband.

"Since I'm here and I saw what happened, it is some of my business, you big over-grown asshole." Derek ignored the look of horror on Raven's features and smirked at the rage on his cousin-in-law's face. He wanted a fight, a good one, and he'd love to whip Thorrason's butt.

When Wulf reached for him, he sidestepped the man, put out one leg, and tripped him. The madder-than-hell thinks-he's-a-Viking went down like a brick house. Derek stood there and gloated until Raven smacked him upside the head.

"How could you? No fair, Derek. You know better than to use your war tactics." She huffed and puffed as she reached down and slid a gentle hand over her husband's shaking body.

The chuckle when it came surprised Derek, and then Wulf whooped with laughter before pulling Raven down for a quick kiss. Once it ended, he pushed her gently away and jumped to his feet. A feat not that easy for a man his size. "Well done, cousin. It's been eons since someone could knock me down without a weapon." Wulf stuck out his hand, then jerked his head toward the back of the house.

"Let's step out for a talk." He gently patted Raven on her backside before speaking. "And I mean *talk*, darling, so take that worried look off your face."

Derek followed his now smiling host to the back porch. The beer in the cooler was a mite warm, but both he and Wulf downed one each before the man spoke again. "I know that you have seen some things that be hard to explain. One of them being me. I know I do not speak as you do, and there is a reason."

"Yeah, you are a bit different than what I thought you'd be like." Derek grinned. "Not in a bad way, but you look like some of the men on the front of the books Raven writes."

"Trust me, not by choice. I mean, I looked this way when I fell into her life."

Wulf's choice of words mystified Derek. "Fell?"

"Yes, and what I be about to tell you is going to sound farfetched, but it be the truth."

"What is it?" Derek was beginning to think Wulf was a few cards short of dealing with a full deck.

Wulf sighed. "It might be better if I just show you." The man stood up, pulled a medallion with a key attached out from under his shirt, and then moved closer to Derek.

Before he could ask if the man was crazy, a hand clamped down on his shoulder, and the world as he knew it dissolved in a mist of black. He shut his eyes, shook his head to ward off an attack of dizziness, and when he opened his eyes again he was standing in what could only be described as a bedchamber. Not like one he'd ever seen except in movies. The room was huge, as was the bed. He turned around, noticed the sweater he'd given Raven last Christmas was hanging on a wooden peg, and then Wulf spoke.

"You will need to change clothes before we can leave this room, and it would be best if you do not speak. Your language is even more present day than Raven's." Wulf moved to an old-looking chest, and pulled out some type of pants and a shirt. "Put these on, and I'll be back to get you in a few minutes."

The man left before Derek could ask him anything, and he had a lot of questions. First off, what had happened back at Raven's? Second, where the hell were they? Derek moved to one of the small windows in the room. He looked down, and his mouth fell open. It was broad daylight outside, men were fighting with swords, and women dressed in antique clothing moved around doing different tasks.

His sensory perception went off radar as he suddenly realized he wasn't in Michigan any longer, and from the look of things, nowhere in present-day America either.

All his life Derek had been programmed to process facts. After college, he entered the military and found he loved working to protect the American people. As special ops, he had to make decisions based on facts and gut instinct. His instinct was telling him now, he needed to get dressed and then get his answers from Wulf. Until then he'd hang tight and wait.

****

Several hours later, he sat in what Wulf called a bathhouse—submerged to his neck in hot water and a horn of mead in his hand. It had taken him a while to realize Wulf wasn't certifiably off his rocker, but in actuality a man who knew how to enjoy the luxuries of life.

Yes, it did freak him out a bit when he realized not only was he in Norway, but in the year 1017. He wondered what the Marine Commandant would think about time travel.

"So I know we time-traveled, but you never said how you ended up in our time." Derek took a sip of the intoxicating brew and bit back a groan. Man, oh man, the Vikings sure knew their liquor.

Wulf's face shone pink in the moonlight streaming in through the only window in the bathhouse. The window was in the back of the wooden structure and looked out over a fiord that he'd been told was similar to a river or lake.

"I don't suppose you would be content in just enjoying the peace and quiet would you?" Wulf spoke from his position on the opposite side of the deep pool. Hot springs supplied the bathwater and benches placed against the sides of the bathing receptacle allowed one or ten at a time to bathe within its depths.

"Hell no. You popped me out of my century, then tell me you and Raven have been going back and forth in time since you two were married, so I want to know how you ended up with my cuz in the first place." Derek took another sip of mead and allowed the hot water to take away some of the tension riding him since the disastrous op in Columbia.

As he watched, the for real, genuine Viking turned the color of a beet. "As you wish. It was Catriona who tossed me into your century."

Derek's head reeled with Wulf's words. What did Catriona have to do with time travel?

"Okay, I'm confused. How does Cat fit into this?" He took another hefty gulp of the brew and waited.

"Since you've embraced time travel, maybe you will believe me when I tell you there are a lot of different entities in this time we're in now and even in yours. Catriona may look like a modern-day woman, but you already know she is different." This time Wulf gulped from his drinking horn before continuing.

"I knew of Catriona before I met her. Of course as a Viking male I thought the stories of fae creatures to be just that, myths handed down from the beginning of time, but I was wrong."

Derek had the feeling Wulf's next words were going to exercise his brain in the impossible and just maybe make him crazy.

"Go on." He drained the last of the mead and then poured some more from a flagon Wulf had given him upon arrival at the bathhouse.

"Catriona is truly a princess. She is a faery princess and she found me taking my pleasure with a woman." Wulf must have noticed Derek's open mouth for he grinned.

"My reputation with women was one of love them and leave them as you would say, but I like to think I always left them feeling happy and satisfied. Evidently that wasn't enough for Catriona. She zapped me, as Raven called it, into the twenty-first century so I could learn the difference between love and lust." Wulf grinned. "She was right. I love Raven like there is no tomorrow."

"Shit, man, you're telling me Cat is really a princess? A faery as in wings and things?" Derek knew he sounded like he was going to lose it, but it wasn't every day he got a chance to tour the eleventh century, find out the woman he was attracted to was a faery creature, and it was just a bit unsettling. He'd rather go one-on-one with an armed terrorist.

"Yes, and that is one of the reasons I was so incensed when I caught you kissing her." His host's lips turned down in a scowl. "You are messing with one vindictive woman if you get on her bad side. Although to be honest, she looked like she liked the kiss." Again Wulf's smile was evident. "In fact she acted like a mortal woman would. But just to be clear, her father is a bit on the possessive side. I think he took umbrage that she helped me and

Raven. Although I'm not certain on that fact."

Derek drained the last of his mead and then sighed. "I don't suppose this is a dream and I'll wake up with just a fractious beautiful woman getting on my last nerve."

"Sorry, but I speak the truth. Just ask Raven."

Before Derek could reply, Raven walked into the bathhouse. Her clothing was that of a Viking woman. She had donned a long dress with a train. The sky-blue color looked good on his cousin, but he knew she wasn't there for compliments.

"Wulf, what are you doing?" Raven's tone was a bit shrill. Not a good sign.

Wulf jumped, then his head went under the water. When he resurfaced, he had a dog-in-trouble look on his face. Who would have thought this man was scared of his wife?

"Raven, my love. What a pleasant surprise."

"Can it, Wulf. Sweet-talk is not going to help you out of this mess. What do you mean by just disappearing off our deck? Now you have opened up an entire can of worms by bringing Derek here." Raven's tone spat fire like a machine gun did bullets. Should he intervene? Naw, let the Viking handle his wife. At the moment, Derek had his own problems. Number one, how to woo a woman who wasn't human.

"Don't rail at me, Raven. You have been telling me since before I met Derek that he is an intelligent person, so I decided he needed to know the truth about us and Catriona."

When Raven opened her mouth again, he admired how Wulf held up his hand and she miraculously stopped.

"Hold, woman. There are some things that are better handled between men. I suggest you go back to our modern home and wait. Derek and I will be there shortly. And pray tell what was the princess doing when you left?"

"I don't know, I didn't talk to her before I left."

"Shit, Raven, you left her alone in our house?" Wulf's use of modern slang shocked Derek, as did his next move. The man shot out of the bath, strode across the floor, and grabbed a robe.

"We have to get back before she lobs fire balls at anything and anyone in her way." Wulf looked back at Derek.

"Calm down, Wulf. Catriona isn't going to hurt anything. Besides, I thought we could stay here for a while." Raven gave him a look that even Derek couldn't miss. It made him want to upchuck at the thought of it being his cousin.

Wulf's grin was a slash of white as he caught her up in his arms. "I think we could wait a bit." He turned back to Derek. "You be all right staying here for a while?"

"Yeah, I'll be fine." Derek waved at Wulf and Raven as they left the bathhouse.

****

Catriona watched from a sliver of moonbeam dancing on the bath's surface. She shouldn't be here, but her angst at being left alone at first by Derek, then Raven, had brought her to this century. Her molecular structure felt strange, probably due to the fact she'd not downsized her body in ages. And although she would look like just a speck of light to anyone glancing her way, her vision remained as it would in a fully sized body. A detail she was exceedingly grateful for since Derek was naked.

She didn't ordinarily drool over men, but there was just something about this green-eyed Marine that made her want to come apart at the wings. Not to mention the broad expanse of naked chest with just a bit of hair narrowing downward to make her want to delve below the water line and explore every sinewy muscle. If she dared, she could have her very own private showing of his manly parts, but what she had in mind would be more fun.

She used her magick to resume her full form but at the same time became invisible. Curiosity had never been one of her faults, and of course she'd never been promiscuous like some of her family, but...

Catriona couldn't resist a closer look at the man who oozed sensuality. She'd been drawn to him ever since he'd stood up to her and refused to give in just because she was considered a beauty.

She liked that he didn't treat her like she was a princess. It was something she could get used to if only...

No use in thinking of the negative, she was a faery, that couldn't be changed, and Derek would be going off to do what he had to do—putting himself in danger, if she read Raven right.

Nothing could come of any type of relationship between them, not that she wanted one. He was a mortal. Certainly not in her class and even if she developed feelings for him, her da would kill him and her before anything came of it. No, better to just be curious and leave the rest of the emotions alone.

Derek jumped when she hesitantly reached out and traced the outline of his manroot with her finger. Lord, that probably wasn't the proper name, but she didn't like calling it some of the terms she'd heard her sister faes use. She pulled back and watched as it got a bit bigger and seemed to stretch. It wasn't as if she hadn't seen one before, she had, but not this close. When she'd caught Wulf in his act of lust before sending him to the twenty-first century, he'd covered himself too quickly for her to get more than a glimpse. And yes some of her fae brothers were good about waving their parts about like they were the best things since magick, but she'd never been interested enough in taking them up on their offer of seeing more. Derek, or his part, was different.

Catriona stifled a giggle as she peered up at his face. His eyes were a bit on the large size as he looked around the room. But then he reclined back against the bathing pool. His lids drifted shut, closing off the green-eyed gaze. Her next move required a bit more courage on her part. She cupped him in her hands and then stroked him from the tip to base.

He jumped even higher this time, and she was rewarded with the firmness under her palms turning into hot steel. Oooh, she never would have thought this part of a man could be soft and hard. Catriona caressed Derek again and received a moan for her administrations.

Before she could find out if it would feel as soft to her lips, Derek abruptly stood up. "I must be losing my mind. No way did someone touch my..." He left the warm cocoon of water, shaking his head. Catriona felt guilty about making him doubt his sanity, but she would do it again in a faery wing sweep if she could. She was a beat away from showing herself to Derek when the bathhouse door opened.

"Raven changed her mind, we are going back to the future." Wulf tossed a robe at Derek and he covered all his luscious and drool-worthy parts. He then walked a bit unevenly across the room.

"Cool by me. I'm more than ready to get back. Just let me get changed."

Catriona wasn't sure why his words hurt as much as they did. It wasn't as if he knew it was she touching him, but all the same it felt like he'd stabbed her just a bit in the region of her heart.

Maybe she would get a chance to talk to him at Raven's. Really talk to him.

The moment the thoughts sealed themselves in

her mind, she realized the mess she'd made before she left.

With one thought, she headed back to the twenty-first century.

Chapter Five

Derek was propelled back to his century and right into chaos. His breath came in gasps, probably from being hurtled through space and time. Soot marks marred the walls and the furniture. While he was gazing around in stunned horror, Raven and Wulf arrived.

"Oh, Princess, what have you done?" Raven's horrified expression effectively stopped Cat's advance into the room. The princess held a bucket in one hand and a sponge in the other.

Her beautiful face wrinkled up and then she began to cry. "I'm sorry, I thought I could get it cleaned up before you got back."

Hell's bells. He hated when they cried. He looked over at Wulf who was having his own problems with a now weeping Raven. Both men shrugged their shoulders, made almost identical grimaces with their lips, and then made their moves. Wulf led Raven up the stairs, and Derek escorted Cat outside after removing the cleaning supplies from her hands. Finally the last of her sniffles dried up, and her shoulders quit shaking. "Cat, you going be okay?"

"What type of question is that?" The princess' snippy tone was back but not as prevalent as before.

"Let me rephrase that: are you going to be still and listen for a moment?" Derek knew his tone was a bit harsh, but it'd been a long day—especially if you counted the daylight hours he'd spent at Wulf's home.

"Why should I?" The haughty tone irritated him, but he did his best to hold his temper. He put a finger under her chin and then raised her face. Her blue eyes were awash with a fresh batch of tears, whether from hurt feelings or temper he didn't know. Her lips were pulled tight, and she gave him a look that dared him to say a word.

"Because Wulf told me what you are." Derek waited for his words to take root. He figured she'd go a bit ballistic, so he held onto her arms, and for good measure he pulled her close to keep her hands from doing any magick.

"So you know I'm not mortal?" Her question surprised Derek. She sounded calm, almost relieved, and even a bit apprehensive.

"Yes." He waited to see what else she would say.

"And?" Catriona's gaze was ripe with uncertainty. He wasn't sure what she wanted him to say. Was he okay with the fact the first woman he'd kissed since his ex-fiancée was a fae creature, as Wulf called her? He didn't have an answer for that one. The events of the afternoon and evening—surely it had been longer?—had been surreal. All he knew for certain was he was tired to the bone.

"I think I need some time to think about that and other things. Can we talk about this in the morning?" Derek eased his grip on Catriona's soft and delightfully curved arms before stepping back.

"I...guess...if that's what you want." Cat's expression was now blank. He hoped he hadn't hurt her feelings. That was one of the last things he wanted.

"It is. Now why don't you try to get some sleep too? 'Night." He didn't wait around to see if she would say anything else, but took the steps two at a time. Once in the guest room he flopped down on the bed without removing his clothes.

And he thought life in the military was hard.

Too many things thrown at him at once only made the tension in the back of Derek's neck worse. He should have gone on R&R some place else. His feelings were all jumbled up, and he didn't need the attraction he felt for a woman, a faery for Heaven's sake, to interfere with getting better. And he certainly shouldn't be thinking about making love to her. Probably the reason he got so hard in the bathhouse. No other reason was possible.

He punched the pillow under his head. He needed to put the last op behind him and get back to being the leader his men expected.

Derek snorted before turning on his side. Some leader. One of his men had died and for that he would never forgive himself. He closed his eyes and tried to shut out the explosion, cries of pain, and above all, the stench of death.

****

Catriona walked back inside and began to clean up the mess she'd made. She should have her wings plucked. Not only had she acted like a faery with an ax to grind, but also in a very childlike manner. All because she'd been left alone.

She would apologize to both Raven and Wulf in the morning, but for now, she'd repair what she'd ruined. She waved her hand and the soot disappeared off furniture. Catriona would physically clean the walls and Raven's personal belongings. It was the least she could do. After thirty minutes of wing-hurting work, she was finished.

Now what to do? She doubted her reluctant and extremely upset hosts would be back down before morning. Derek... Well, all she could say about him was she was clueless. No man had ever treated her like he did. At first with derision, then with a commanding air, and then a kiss that singed her wings. But that was before he found out she was fae. Any chance of...what? What did she want from him?

And why did she want him?

The mortal was irritating, rude, but he did make her feel like a woman and not a princess. And oh, how she loved touching him. What would it feel like if she actually allowed him to see her while she indulged her curiosity? Would he make love to her? And if he did where would they go from there? Would he take her seriously if she said she'd like to explore a relationship with him? No one else took her seriously. Only when her fae family and friends wanted something would they treat her like she had any sense. The rest of the time, Catriona was deemed to be a bit eccentric. And why was she even thinking of having any type of relationship with Derek? She knew the rules. No fae should have contact with mortals. Or that was what her father kept telling Catriona.

Catriona swiped at her eyes. The military macho Marine had succeeded in giving her back something she had lost: a sense of self. Her da, bless his heart, was more likely to pat her on the head, tell her to whip up something beautiful to wear, and then send her to the outer reaches of the Seelie Court for vacation with a guardian.

Centuries of being treated like a pampered little fae girl had turned her into a spoiled and in some cases vindictive woman. Wulf had been the recipient of the duress left over from a fight with her sister. If Celine had not been so snotty about a piece of jewelry Catriona had borrowed, then she wouldn't have thrown in her face the fact her daughter was nothing more than a slut—sleeping with mortals and immortals alike. Now that's when her father should have done something. Cat's niece should have been punished. It was only right since Catriona was barred from mixing with mortals. Yet, when the high and mighty Celine went crying to their da, he'd sent Catriona to punish Wulf, which she did, only not in

42

the way her family wanted.

Maybe she should have kept her mouth from flapping like her wings but if she had then Wulf and Raven wouldn't have met one another, and in her opinion that would be a hundred times worse than her interference. They truly had found a love that surpassed time.

Catriona threw a pillow from the couch across the room, and then snatched it back with a flick of her fingers. Yes, she was a woman and she needed to change if she ever wanted to have what Raven did with Wulf. Could she find that with Derek? Did she want to try?

She eased even farther down on the couch. The throw pillow now pressed under her cheek. She needed to think about what she wanted and the way she wanted to go.

And if I decide to go after Derek and win him, then what? Will I be willing to stand up to my da, the king?

Catriona shut down the offensive and frightening thought as quickly as it came.

****

A faint moan woke Catriona up. As she tried to blink the sleep from her eyes, she heard the sound again. It came from directly overhead. After moving her stiff body off the offending couch, she transported herself upstairs. She stopped outside Raven and Wulf's door but sensed no presence on the inside. They may have gone back to his home. She then moved down the hallway to a guest room next to hers—Derek's room.

The noise came again and she eased the door open. Derek's fine body lay sprawled on top of the covers. As she waited to see if he moaned again, he twisted and turned. His face was all screwed up in a grimace. Could he be in pain? She moved to the bed and then lightly touched his forehead with her palm.

43

The dream hit her so hard she staggered backward. So much pain, physically and emotionally. How could Derek endure it? She should wake him, but when she reached forward to shake him, he spoke.

"Mitch, you okay, man?" His tone was rushed, anguished even, and Catriona, knowing she would regret it, put her hand back on his face.

Derek hunkered down behind a tall Brazilian nut tree and tried to assess the damage. His unit had been tracking a cell of supposed terrorists into the Columbian jungle when they were jumped from behind. All hell broke loose. Mitchell, a man who'd been with Derek since he'd made special ops, had fallen like a downed tree. Derek couldn't tell if he was dead or alive. Joe, Derek's second in command, was pinned down on the other side of the trail. He'd taken a hit also but was still able to communicate by hand gestures.

He thumbed the button on his Sataphone. Static greeted his ears, but he had to try. "Michigan Fox to base. Michigan Fox to base. We are taking fire."

No voice came back to him. "I repeat. We are taking fire. Michigan Fox and kits under attack."

"Repeat. We are under fire. Need transport." Derek looked across the road and motioned for Joe to stay put. Stevens, the fourth in their group, crouched down a few yards from Joe. Anders, the final special ops Marine, lay stretched out on his stomach about ten feet from Mitchell's body.

Thank God no one else had taken a hit. The entire operation had been cursed from the beginning. The intel as to where the terrorists were located had been wrong and only by an act of God had they found the one member of the cell who was willing to divulge info.

Derek wanted to kick his own ass. He should have known something was up. But he wanted to do his job, to stop the cell from growing spurs in the states like intel inferred they would.

Several minutes passed and he had a choice to make—stay there until someone could get them out, or forge forward. Dammit, he was a Marine. He wasn't going to cower, and he didn't want to take a chance they'd be hit after dark from all sides. Better to move now if possible, but which way?

A slight moan came from behind him. Mitchell was still alive. That settled it. They needed to get to the next available city and hospital. He looked toward Joe, and motioned toward the trail. Joe would pass the plan on to the others. In the meantime, he had to get to Mitch. The restoration of birds chirping and squirrels scampering in the overhead branches, gave credence to the thought their attackers had struck and moved on.

Not something he would have done, his unit would have tried to capture their quarry, extract info, and the fact they'd been left alone after the initial attack made him think the group had bigger fish to fry.

Derek shifted his gear to one shoulder, slid down on his belly, and made his way to Mitch. He checked his stats and prayed the hole in his chest wasn't as damaging as it looked. He took off his shirt and stuffed it into what was left of Mitch's shirt. Hopefully it would contain the bleeding until they could get him to a doctor.

He came up in a crouch, scooped the injured man up and over his shoulder before rising to his feet. His men were checking the perimeters and then gathered close to him.

"Okay guys, we have no choice but to go straight ahead. I want to get Mitch some help."

"Yeah, too bad we had to leave Jacob behind because of that busted leg." The medic who usually accompanied them had fallen down a flight of stairs right before they were scheduled to go belly up. The replacement they were suppose to have had never happened.

"I know. Let's move out." Derek didn't waste time on bemoaning what had happened, he needed to make sure that nothing else happened on his watch. They kept their pace steady, alert to anything that would signify the terrorists' possible return.

A while later, Derek pulled out his compass. They were only a few klicks from the town. He didn't allow himself a breath of relief. He would not rest easy until Mitch was taken care of, the mission finished, and his men safe back stateside.

By now the sun had started to go down, and the shadows from the trees interspersed the trail with semi-darkness. Not the best scenario, but one that had to be dealt with—Mitch had not moaned once in the last hour. Time was running out. As Derek continued to move forward he heard the rustle of the bushes on either side of the trail before hell erupted.

Chapter Six

Catriona pulled out of Derek's mind and dream so quickly she staggered back toward the window. Her hands were shaking, and her head reeled with the images of blood and death.

She tried to block the dream's remnants and focus on Derek who was thrashing around on the bed. The look on his face even more horrific than before as he remained caught in the nightmare.

He needed to be awakened and quickly. Catriona retraced her steps, reached out and gently touched his shoulder, and found herself propelled through the air to land on the bed—Derek's body holding her down.

"Derek, wake up."

She didn't get any response.

"Derek, please...you must wake up. Now!" Catriona used a slight touch of magick to reinforce her command. She was rewarded when his lids lifted and his green eyes looked down at her, at first with confusion and then horror.

"Oh God above, Cat. I'm sorry." He rolled off her body, and she wished to have him back.

"It's okay. You were having a nightmare." Catriona kept her tone soft. He still looked spooked enough to do anything.

Derek scrubbed a hand over his eyes and then pushed off the bed. He wasn't sure what had happened. The dream had been ten times worse this time. Why? And why was Catriona in his room?

"What are you doing in here?" He moved to the

window before turning back to look at Catriona, who now stood near the door.

"I heard you. I mean the sounds you made in your dream. I thought I could help." Her gaze held caution, and pity if he wasn't mistaken.

"How could you help? And what do you know about my dream?"

Derek closed the distance between them and grabbed her arm.

"Let me go, mortal. You're hurting me." Her cry only incensed him. She wasn't human, she could never be his even if he wanted a lasting relationship, and she had invaded his dreams. He knew that, just as he knew Mitch was dead and gone.

"What did you do? Snoop inside my head while I slept?" He shook her, and she flung her hand up. The wave of electricity tossed him a few feet away. He shook his head to dispel the effect of her magick.

"No, I didn't just dive inside your thoughts. I tried to quiet you and got pulled into them. And just because you're a mortal, doesn't mean you can mistreat someone." Cat waved her hand. Her body began to waver and he lunged for her arm once again.

"Cat, please, don't go. I'm sorry."

"Ha! Why should I believe you?" Her blue gaze pinned him in place, but at least she didn't shake off his hand.

"Because, I am truly sorry. I get a bit ballistic about someone messing around in my head. The company shrink did enough of that after we got back from Columbia." His voice trembled just a bit, and he hoped Cat didn't notice. *Nothing like showing you're a spineless wimp around a woman.*

"I'm sorry too. I wouldn't have gone into your thoughts but you looked so distressed." Catriona gazed up at him. "I am sorry about your friend, and about all that happened to you and your men."

Derek wasn't sure what to say. After his atrocious attitude, she still felt pity for him. And while he wouldn't take sympathy from just anyone, coming from the princess it felt kinda right.

"Thanks. It was a bad time. Mitch was a good man, and he'll be missed." Derek moved back. He needed to distance himself. Cat's eyes were pulling him into a place he didn't want to go. No, make that couldn't go. She was a fae princess, out of his league. Derek grimaced. Out of his world. He could never make her part of his, and he doubted she would ever be happy living the life of a military wife. If it even got that far.

"Derek, what's wrong?" Cat's question reminded him of the here and now. And the present reality that he was a Marine who would be returning to duty in just a few weeks.

"Uh, nothing. I appreciate you being concerned, but I'm fine."

"I don't think so. How could you be?" Cat's continued concern touched him but...

"Please don't shut me out. I just want to help."

"You think I'm trying to shut you out? Cat, you have no idea what I'm trying to do, or want." Derek bit out the words.

"Then why don't you tell me?"

Cat's question wasn't meant to inflame him but it did.

"How about I show you instead?" Before he changed his mind, he pulled her into his arms and staked claim to her lips. She opened to him as she had before.

Her tongue dueled with his, and he sampled all she had to give and then more. His hands were not idle either. He reached into the neckline of her gown and touched what lay beneath. Her breasts fit so perfectly in his palms, and he wanted to taste them. Derek reluctantly removed his lips from Cat's, but the first taste of one nipple caused his rod to harden even more. He licked, nipped, then kissed his way around her aureole, before switching to the other beckoning offering.

"Derek? I've never felt like this before." Catriona's whispered words ended on a moan.

How on earth could a woman as beautiful as she was never have been loved?

"No one has ever made you moan, babe?" He transferred his attention to other parts of her body.

"Never. In fact, you're the first man to truly kiss me." Cat's admission stunned Derek so much so he almost stopped running his hands up and down her hips.

"Unbelievable. Are the men in your realm blind?"

Cat's giggle caressed his heart.

"No. They have tried, but I've never been interested in the men in my realm, or for that fact in the mortal world, until you. And besides, my da is a bit of a stickler for his daughters to be chaste until they choose their mates."

Whoa, did she say chaste and mate? Derek's heart thudded at the thought if he took her he'd be her first, and he wasn't at all sure he was ready for a mate. If that was even possible with Cat.

Before he could make up his mind to continue or send Cat away, she took matters into her own hands. The soft touch of her palm as it slid over the rigid hardness bowed up against his zipper took away every thought in his head except sinking deep inside this woman's body.

First, however, he wanted to send her up in flames, taste the dew of her desire, and then bring her to climax once again while he thrust into her wet center.

His hands, which had stilled upon hearing her words, finished stripping the dress off her supple body. His gaze found and held every valley, curve, and line of her luscious frame, before he began a slow exploration. And all the time his hands moved, so did Cat's. Her touch was sending him over the edge, and he needed to reel her in before he lost it— when he came he wanted to be deep inside Catriona.

He took one of his hands and captured both of hers.

"No, Derek, I want to touch you." Cat's words were a benediction on his bruised soul. He needed someone to touch him, and touch him badly. He'd tried women in the past as a conduit to rid himself of the emotional baggage after returning home from a mission, but without allowing them too close. It hadn't worked. Yet with Cat he felt something besides the need to vanquish his nightmares.

"Don't move." He wasn't sure if she would do as he asked or not, or even if he wanted her to, but he planned to conquer every unbreached territory he could find. Derek started at her neck, trailing kisses down the slender column of her throat. The moans she emitted were music to his starved heart. He retraced the path to her breasts, and then watched her eyes go a sapphire blue.

Catriona didn't know if she would live through the sweet torture Derek inflicted on her love-starved body. Never in a millennium had anyone ignited a flame so hot, so bone melting, and so welcomed. His tongue tickled her as it assaulted her senses and made her crave more. His mouth was a hot vacuum against her nipples as he blew, licked, and then suckled them until they ached with need.

His hair fell forward and tickled her midsection as he moved slowly down her body. Derek's breath on her center shot Catriona's hips off the bed. She grabbed his head and held him still for a moment as his gaze touched hers. The smirk on his lips implied he knew she liked it. And he was right.

When his fingers slid through the hair at the apex of her thighs, she couldn't stop her whimper.

"You like that don't you?" Derek's teasing tone only ratcheted her desire up a few degrees.

"Yes...now please stop teasing me." Catriona wanted to groan as he slowly pulled his hand back, and then she did when his thumb and forefinger encircled the center of her ache.

"Oh, I plan to tease you until you cry out for mercy, Cat. And you'll love every second." Derek's breath caressed her flesh and her hips left the mattress again. So not fair. She wanted to touch him, and she could if she used her magick. Catriona wanted to but then decided she'd rather their first time be his way.

The touch of his tongue caused her heart to skip and then bang against her chest wall. Her body undulated as she tried at first to get away from the electrifying strokes. But then she began to feel the most enticing sensation as tiny bands of fire grew tighter and tighter inside her female core.

Catriona pushed her hips closer to Derek's lips. She needed something, anything, to make the hurt stop. A long, slow stroke followed by the sharp nip of his teeth, and her body convulsed into spasm after spasm of heat until she thought she'd pass out.

Derek crawled up her body and then almost kissed her senseless. "Now, it's my turn," he growled when he released her lips. He then moved off the bed and discarded his clothes, before climbing between her thighs. Catriona waited for him to claim her as his. The aftermath of her climax had turned her limbs into useless appendages. The only part of her body not limp with sated desire was her heart, which continued to beat at an accelerated rate.

Catriona forced her arms up; she wanted to hold Derek close as he made her a woman, his woman. She knew he would be the only man for her. No fae male could equal him and she would never take one of her own kind for a lover. Not now and not ever. She didn't care what the rules of the Seelie Court were, if she had to and Derek wanted her, she would give up her place as a princess.

Derek grinned down at her, his lips a sensual temptation when he pushed closer. She closed her eyes and waited—only to hear words that frightened her almost out of her wings.

Catriona, I'm home. The king, her da's voice inside her head shook her from her lassitude.

"Oh my stars and constellations." Her shriek elicited a response from Derek.

"Not yet, but you will see all kinds of heavenly bodies, and that's a promise." Derek's lips hovered an inch from Cat's. What to do? She didn't want to leave him. Could she just ignore the king?

Catriona, where are you? His tone, which had been congenial, now carried a hard edge. *You better not be anywhere near the mortal realm.*

Before she could change her mind, she concentrated on her room at home, a change of clothes, and then with a wave of her hand she was gone.

Chapter Seven

Catriona ran down the corridor to the throne room. A servant had been sent to roust her from her bedroom. And thank the muses she'd been there when Malik, one of her da's house faes, had knocked on her door. It had been close, and now she had to face off with her da, and she prayed to the God Raven knew that he would not keep her from going back to Derek.

"Catriona, it's about time. What took you so long, daughter?" King Tiernan, as most of the Seelie Court called him, intimidated a lot of the fae males. His stature was large, strong, and muscular. And it seemed they thought him to be a rival for the women of the court. And although Cat didn't see her da as anything but her da, she supposed his hair, a darker shade than Catriona's silver tresses, could be considered an attribute. The crown he wore low on his forehead accented his bronze skin, and made the blue of his eyes more prominent. Yes, his looks could be considered something women would like. His deep baritone growl would be off putting to the males, but never to Catriona.

She didn't fear her da's bark as much as she dreaded disappointing him. Yes, she did things he didn't like and when caught she fought the restraints of his and the Seelie Court's rule. Now she needed to placate him. Convince him she was fine and then get back to Derek. No way could she imagine how he felt when she just disappeared without a word. Yet she couldn't take the chance her da would track her down in the mortal world. All the military weapons made would not keep Derek safe if her da found them together.

"I'm sorry. I felt the need to freshen up just a bit. You're home early." She walked to the king and then placed a quick kiss on his cheek.

"Why do I believe there is more than just you wanting to change clothes? What have you been up to while I was gone?" His questions were pleasant enough but she knew he would delve inside her thoughts if she didn't satisfy his curiosity.

"A bit of this and a bit of that. Actually, I am thinking of redecorating the palace. It's beginning to look a bit frayed." Catriona inserted a good amount of boredom in her tone.

"If you're bored then you might be interested in going with me when I visit our neighboring realm." Her da's statement sounded like a trap. Catriona would need to exercise caution to get out of whatever he planned.

She reclined in the matching throne chair. Since her da had never remarried, she and Celine were the only ones allowed to utilize her mother's seat. "So where did you plan to go and on what business?" She held one hand up, studied her nails, and kept her mind blank.

"I thought we'd visit Alex's court. His oldest son is home from touring the universe and wishes to take a mate." The king's eyes turned a darker blue as his gaze speared Catriona.

"Whilst this might be more fun than having my wings plucked, I have no desire to be mauled by Adam." Catriona gave her da one of his own looks back.

"He dared touch you, my daughter?" His words were a testament of his angst. Possibly she'd opened up a bottle of concern that needed to be capped.

"No, he never got a chance, but that is why I do

not wish to accompany you. I'll just stay here."
Catriona hoped he would drop the subject.

"I don't like leaving you alone so much. Perhaps I will postpone the trip or get Celine to stay with you."

"No!" Her statement caused her da to raise an eyebrow. Oh mercy, she needed to redirect his thoughts.

"What I mean is this trip is important to you, and Celine has just gotten back to her home. No need to bring her here. I will be fine." She hazarded a glance toward the king. He looked disturbed but not overly so. Hopefully she could pull this off or she'd end up with her own wings pulled.

"I don't like it, but when I return we will discuss you finding a mate. Celine is happy with the mate I chose for her."

Catriona snorted. "Of course she's happy with Corsair, he allows her to do anything she wants, and that goes for her slutty daughter too."

"Catriona! Do not talk about your niece that way. She is young and will learn." Her da moved down the steps of the dais and walked in front of where she was sitting.

"Young, my wings. She is way old enough to show respect, and she doesn't. I know for a fact she seduces anyone she sets her gaze upon." Cat spit out the words, and then drew up a bit. She could be lighting a fire she couldn't quench.

"I know she is a bit..."

"Wild?" Catriona tossed out.

"Yes, but so was her mother. You, however, have always been the obedient one. Gentle and kind, like my dear, sweet Alisanne. I'm afraid your sister took after me when it comes to the lustful side of our fae nature." Tiernan stopped in front of Catriona. "This is why I want to see you take a mate, Catriona. Too many times you have sneered, turned down, or humiliated suitors. You need a mate in order to take your place as my heir and future ruler."

She couldn't believe her ears. Rule the Tuatha de Danann?

"Da, I can't be a ruler. It should be a male."

Tiernan's smile lacked humor. "Maybe so, Catriona, but your mother and I were never blessed with a son, and I refuse to mate again. You are my oldest, and will rule when I'm gone."

Although there were times she wished her da far away, Catriona had never thought of a life or world without him. Fae males lived millennia. Why would he think she would ever need to rule?

"Da, do not talk nonsense. You will rule our people for several more millennia. There will never be a reason for me to take over, and I don't want to hear anymore about this." Catriona got up and did something she rarely did, slid her arms around her da's waist, and gave him a hug.

"Catriona, don't worry child, I don't plan on dying just yet, but..."

"No buts. Now, lets go have dinner and then you can tell me about your trip." She did want to know what her da had been up to, but a part of her grieved she could not be with Derek. And she worried he would never forgive her for leaving him in the state he was in when she just disappeared.

****

Derek fell on the bed and turned sideways just in time to prevent damaging his hard-on. Where did Cat go? And more importantly how in the hell could she leave right when he was ready to plunge inside her depths?

Women! You couldn't trust them to follow through with anything. And to think he'd almost began to care for Catriona. Yes, it was against his code to allow another close to him, not after Lisa, but somehow the little faery had slid right under his radar.

Now look at him. Left at the breach point, hurting like hell, and no rhyme or reason for any of the events he'd experienced since coming to Raven's. Derek reached down and grasped his hardware in one hand. He could finish the job without Catriona, but it wouldn't be the same. Instead he rolled off the bed and pulled on his jeans before leaving the bedroom.

A couple of beers later, he sat at the kitchen table still bemoaning how devious the female race could be, when Raven and Wulf zapped into the room.

"Derek, I thought you'd be asleep." Raven glanced his way before moving to the refrigerator. She pulled out a pitcher of water and poured a glass. When she pointed the pitcher at him and Wulf, they both shook their heads.

"I was asleep but decided to get up." What else could he say? That he was on the verge of screwing their other houseguest when she disappeared? No, better to let it go and then get the hell out Michigan as fast as he could. He'd go back to base and recover there. Although austere, it beat the hell out of staying in his apartment.

"Nightmares?" Raven's soft tone was sympathetic, and he loved her for caring, but would prefer not to get into it with her.

"Yeah, but they're gone. And I think it's time I do the same." He caught the hand she held out to him.

"Don't go, Derek. You still need time to heal."

"Some things don't ever heal, and you know it, cuz." He squeezed her hand, exchanged a look with Wulf, and then stood up.

"I can kick back at the base, and then be ready to go when they need me." Derek hated leaving this way, but with his feelings all out of whack when it came to Cat, he needed the space.

"I wish..." Raven's voice trailed off.

"He knows what he's doing, Raven." Wulf looked at Derek. "You are welcome here any time."

Derek grinned. Quite a turnaround since he first darkened their threshold.

"Thanks, cuz!" He threw a salute toward his family and headed for the stairs. No time like the present to throw stuff in his duffel bag and get going.

He decided to forego a shower and proceeded to toss all his clothes into the oversized canvas bag. Good thing Rav had washed clothes before Cat's unexpected arrival. It would save him the trouble of doing it himself.

Derek moved into the bathroom and started hauling out his shaving gear and other toiletry items. He stashed them into a smaller bag and placed it inside the larger one. He was at the point of grabbing his comb when the room shimmered with color.

"Derek, why are you leaving?" Catriona's question showered him with all kinds of emotions. The foremost? Anger.

"Why? You don't know?" He pulled on his shirt, stuffed his feet into sneakers, and then hoisted the duffel onto his shoulder. He purposely ignored how sexy she looked in the princess garb she wore. The flowing dress looked like a blue-green sea with the long skirts trailing the floor. The crown—God above, were those diamonds?—looked like it was made for Cat.

"No, I don't understand. I know—"

"Know what? That you left me at a time most men would kill a woman for leaving? That you're nothing but a tease? Do you even know what that word means?" He didn't care if he was yelling. He had a right to his rage. The right of a man hung out to dry without any satisfaction.

"I couldn't help it. My da got home and I didn't want him—"

"To know his daughter was going to have sex? Well, couldn't you have said something before you just popped out?" Unreasonable he might be, and still more than a bit riled, he did understand irate dads could be a bit nasty.

"I was afraid if I said anything, he'd follow my voice and find me—us. I didn't want that to happen." Catriona worried her upper lip with her teeth and gave Derek a look that almost melted his angst.

"I suppose he might have been a tad upset if he'd found us naked."

"Oh yes, more than a bit. In fact you probably wouldn't have liked what he'd turn you into." Catriona looked a bit frightened, and that scared the crap out of Derek.

"Seriously? He'd actually change me into another person, creature, etc." His mouth stayed open as she nodded her head.

"That and more. He might even curse you so you could never have sex again." She moved a bit closer to him. "And I think that would be horribly sad."

"You and me both, sister." Derek raked a hand through his hair, and resisted the urge to touch his hardware.

"So, are we okay, as Raven says?" Catriona moved closer and stretched her hand toward Derek. He felt like a heel. The woman hadn't just left him to play games; she thought she was protecting him. He could understand that.

"Yeah, we're okay." He tossed the duffle on the bed. The next moment his arms were full of Cat. "Just promise me, if we get to that point again, you won't just leave without notice?"

Cat smiled up at him. "I promise."

He lowered his head for a kiss.

"Derek?"

"Yeah?"

He didn't really want to talk; he'd rather kiss her.

"I have never felt like I do with you when I've been with the fae males. Why is that, do you know?"

Whoa.

Her question threw him for a loop.

What did she feel and should they even be talking about feelings? It would lead to nowhere. He had his duty, and she wasn't human.

"I don't know, babe. It's kinda hard to say." He straightened, dropped his arms from around her slender waist, and stepped back.

"Well, I know that all the men my da has tried to mate me with do not make me feel all jittery inside. I know mortals call that love, and even though I told Wulf he needed to learn the difference in that and lust, how do you know if it's one or the other?" Cat's words hit him hard—in the heart and mind.

"Mate? Your dad is trying to mate you with someone?" Of all the questions he had after her dropped bomb, that was the one he wanted answered first and then he would ask the second most important.

Catriona sat down on the edge of the bed. "Yes, but so far I've turned down every suitor. I don't want to marry someone who only wants to rule the Seelie Court after my da..."

"After your da dies? I didn't know faeries could." Derek was more confused than ever.

"Maybe I should just tell you a bit about my people." She patted the bed.

Derek took a seat. "Yeah, that would probably be best."

"The Tuatha de Danann go back so far in the world's history even we don't know when we were created. There are two parts to my people. The Seelie Court, who strive to do no wrong, and the UnSeelie Court, who love stirring up mischief, mayhem, and anything else that will hurt someone."

Cat laughed. "I think some of my family should have been delegated to that realm. But for the most part we just live and love. There are mates, like your husbands and wives, children, and a life that is surrounded by mystical and glorious things."

Catriona looked up at him. "I grew bored with the day-to-day existence. I wanted to see more of the other worlds. To experience life as someone other than a princess. And over the centuries, I've learned that not all mortals are shallow, mindless creatures, who live for pleasure and to hurt others."

Derek reached out and caught her hand in his but remained silent.

"A lot of your people try to do good and turn their eyes toward what you call Heaven. A God that loves all. That, to a fae, is unbelievable. We believe in ourselves and the king. However, I like the idea that there is one entity that cares for others and although I know not all of your people pray, it is refreshing to find there is goodness and mercy also in this realm of yours."

Catriona gave a bit of a laugh. "I'm sorry, I digress. My people are ancient, we've seen the Druids come and go, witch-hunts, wars, and other equally horrid events, but through it all we have for the most part stayed separate. My da scared me tonight. He talked about a time when he might not be around to rule."

"Everyone dies." Derek wasn't sure how his words would be taken, but he hoped Cat would understand he wanted to help.

"That's just it, Derek. Faeries, or at least not the fae I know, don't die. They tend to drift away from the court and we never hear from them again. For my da to talk about actually losing his life is unrealistic to me, as well as devastating. What he told me is, I have to choose a mate in order to rule after him."

Derek couldn't stop the flame throw of jealously eating his insides.

"So have you chosen your mate?"

Chapter Eight

"No, I have not. There is no one in my realm that makes me feel like you do. And since it is forbidden for me to take a mate that is not fae, then I don't plan to marry at all."

Catriona's heart broke as she uttered the words. Her life would be an endless berth of loneliness if she stuck to her plan. Yet, how could she marry another when she was in love with Derek? Of course the emotion was new, but from what she'd read, love meant you put that person first, wanted the absolute best for them, and would do anything to make sure they were safe.

"Cat, I don't know what to say. I can't even think about what that would mean for you. But at the moment, I know I want to love you like there is no tomorrow. But I think we both need some time to think about what we feel." Derek's voice came right above her left ear, and she leaned into his body.

"I know you are right, but for some reason, I don't like it." Catriona sighed.

"If it helps, Princess, neither do I." Derek's gaze caught hers. "Life isn't always what we want. And it has a way of getting in the way of desires." This time Derek sighed. "I will have to go back to my base sooner than later, and then be assigned to my next mission. There is no place in my life for anyone. Being a Marine is all I've ever wanted to do, and I still want to serve my country, yet, for the first time I'm finding there might be more than mission after mission."

"So what do we do?" Her question was a plea straight from her heart. She wanted more time to find out if this truly was love. And if so, then there had to be someway they could stay together—without upsetting her da or the faery realm.

Derek frowned and then a smile lit his sensual lips. "Let's go for a walk." He motioned toward the window where weak sunshine now crept through. While they had been talking the sun had risen.

"All right. If that's what you want." Catriona wasn't all that keen on just walking for the sake of the motion. She preferred a faster mode of transportation, but if it made him happy then she was willing.

"Good, but you need to change clothes. Although you look beautiful in that getup, you need something warmer."

Derek was right. The weather in the mortal realm, although Spring, was much colder than at home. She waved her hand and her faery garb was transformed into a pair of jeans, sweater, socks, and low boots.

"Wow, that was something else." Derek's eyes were wide as he gazed at Catriona. She supposed she could have gone to her room and changed there, but she didn't really want to waste the time she might have with Derek.

"Yes, magick comes in handy at times." She grinned at him, and then caught his hand. "Now let's go for that walk."

****

A couple of hours later, Derek was ready to kick himself. Although the walk had been fruitful in gathering more information about Catriona's world, he still had no idea what to do about her or his lust. The more they walked with her huddled right under his arm, a position he really could get used to, the more he wanted her physically. Yet, did he have the

65

right to take what belonged to her mate? Yes, even if she swore she would never marry, she could change her mind, and he didn't want to be labeled her first lover and nothing else.

Dammit. How could he have fallen in love with a faery? Even as that thought settled in his mind, another one followed. How could he not? Catriona, the real Cat, was sweet, kind, funny, loving, and oh-so-desirable. And Derek felt like a mouse trying to escape a predator. He had this soul-shattering feeling that no matter what the future brought, he would never be shed of his feelings for Catriona.

"Derek, there is a noise coming from your jeans." Cat's tone, a bit apprehensive as well as curious stirred him from his thoughts. His cell phone, which he'd set on vibrate, rumbled.

"It's my phone. Hang on a minute. I have to see who it is." He pulled the phone out, and bit back a groan as he saw his commanding officer's number flashing back at him.

He slapped the phone to his ear. "Sir, Harrison here, sir."

"Derek, forget the formality. I hate to take you off of R&R but we have an emergency."

His radar pinged as he heard the unspoken concern in Commander Gentry's voice.

"Yes, sir. Where should I go and when?" He wondered if his other men had been notified.

"Nowhere. Your men will be coming to you. There is intel chatter that homegrown terrorist are going to release a toxic chemical into the Great Lakes. If successful, it will contaminate the water supply into Canada, and down the Eastern seaboard. They must be stopped."

Derek's head reeled with the possible repercussions. Not since the nineties had there been such a potent threat by terrorists who claimed America as their country. A slow burn began in his veins as he listened to where he needed to go after his crew got there. His mind was already choreographing the steps they needed to take.

"Good luck, Derek. Stay safe."

"Thank you, Commander. Will do. And I'll contact you when the mission's accomplished." Derek closed his phone and stood there for a moment. The implications of what could happen put a fear in his heart he didn't need. Now was the time to act, to stop the men who would defile their homeland soil. Their goal to kill thousands of Americans, and even if he and his men could contain the pollution to one lake it would still be catastrophic. No, the threat had to be stopped before it happened.

"Derek, what's wrong?" So involved in the moment, he'd forgotten Catriona was there.

"I have to leave, Princess. A job's come up that has to be handled right away." He grabbed her hand and tugged her back to Raven's and then up the stairs. There he retrieved his duffle and headed for the door only to stop with his hand out to turn the knob.

"Look," he said as he angled his body to face Cat. "I'm not sure how long I'll be gone. Will you be here when I get back?"

"I might be at the Seelie Court." Catriona removed a thin chain from underneath her sweater. "Put this on, it will insure I hear you if you call me." Catriona moved closer and handed him the circle of silver.

"Okay, thanks." He looped the chain around his neck, leaned down, and caught her lips with his. He savored the sweet taste the kiss brought. Derek hated leaving this way, but, and that was a very slim but, if she and he were to become an item Cat would have to learn what his life as a Marine really entailed.

He pulled back from the kiss and left the room

without a word.

****

Catriona watched Derek leave and wished she could call him back. The glimpse she'd had of his life as a Marine frightened her. And now she felt even more terrified. She could help him if he would allow her to. She'd heard what the Commander told him, and although she knew it was wrong to use her magick that way, she couldn't resist finding out where Derek was going.

The thought he could suffer pain again of any kind was abhorrent to her. Derek had experienced enough. She didn't understand why he wanted to do a job that could get him killed, but men it seemed were the same, mortal or fae. Stubborn and all male. Not a good combination when it came to making life choices in her opinion.

Unsure of what to do with herself and not wanting to leave, even for a bit, without saying goodbye to her hosts, she flashed to the kitchen. Raven sat with her head cupped on her hands, Wulfgar stood behind her patting her back.

"Hello."

Both turned toward her, and Catriona shivered at the look of misery in Raven's eyes. She wondered if half of what she felt shone from hers.

"Catriona, we didn't know if you were still here or not."

"Yes, I was with Derek when he received his phone call." Catriona moved to Raven. "I'm sorry. I wish that I could do something to help."

"I know you do, but Derek is so stubborn he won't admit he's not ready to go back out. He needs more time to recuperate." Raven took the hand Catriona offered.

"Raven, you know Derek has a job to do. I understand your worry, but he is not a swaddling babe to be protected." Wulf's insertion did not make either one of them feel better if Raven's trembling hand was an indication.

Catriona blinked the moisture gathering in her eyes. "No, but he needs to be kept safe. I know you think I'm nothing but a worthless piece of fluff. That I live to make mischief and to please myself, Wulfgar, but that is not true. I realize the implications of Derek's job. I've been inside his nightmares. They are not pretty. I just don't want him hurt."

"Was it bad?" Raven's timid question broke Catriona's own self-pity. Could she speak of what she'd seen? The blood, the carnage, when they were attacked the second time. If Derek had not told her then neither would she.

"Bad enough. I gave Derek a necklace. If he calls me I will hear him. I hope and pray to the mortal God that he will do so if he gets into trouble."

Catriona eased her hand from Raven's. "I need to go and check in with my da. He is home now, and will expect to see me until he leaves on another visit to the outer reaches of our court." She waved her hand and handed a chain similar to the one she'd given Derek to Raven. "If you need me, put this on, and call my name." She nodded to Wulf and then flashed herself to the Seelie Court.

****

Derek watched from the outer banks of Lake Michigan where it dissected with its sister lakes, Huron and Superior. This would be, in his opinion, the place the terrorists would strike first. With all five of the water tributaries connected, the terrorists would only have to pollute one to have a devastating effect on the States and the world.

His men were hunkered down at hundred foot intervals, including Mitch's replacement. Sam James had the experience Derek wanted to fit in with his group, and a quick wit, but he also had a serious side that would make him an asset.

They would maintain silence until they spotted their quarry. It was night and although it would be easier to blend in during the day, Derek's instinct told him these traitors to America would strike in the dark. Not wanting their identities to be known. Only if their actions bore fruit would they proclaim their victory by allowing officials to know who they were. He just prayed they could stop them before it was too late.

A fox scampered near him, seeing Derek as nothing but an immovable object in the night. As long as the wildlife remained calm, then he knew the terrorists were not near. And having the furry creature approach could be a good sign, since Derek's nickname on maneuvers was Michigan Fox.

He changed his position just a bit to ease the cramp in his leg. A limb that had suffered serious injury from the debacle in Columbia. He'd never told Raven about the weeks of surgery he'd undergone or the rehab he'd endured to get his leg back up to par. No need for his sweet cousin to know he'd almost bled out before help had arrived. His men had also suffered extensive injuries but by the "Ooohrahs" and the grins when they'd met at the airport, all of them, Joe, Anders, and Stevens were in high spirits and ready to do their jobs. Jacob had even returned to the unit, and as much as he hated the thought they might need a medic, he was glad to have him back.

An owl's hoot sounded above, and the slight moonlight highlighted the massive bird's wingspan. This was their second night on watch, and intel chatter indicated the terrorists were on the move. An inside source who was reputed to have infiltrated this cell months before had managed to get that information to Homeland Security before they left wherever they were holed up.

He couldn't wait to take down the terrorists and get back to Catriona. There was a lot of unfinished business he wanted to nail down. The first one being her luscious body, and then he'd move on to how deep their feelings were for one another, and after that he would tackle the daddy issue. Surely one Marine could take on a faery male and win. At least he hoped so.

A sudden flight of birds, followed by several rustlings in the brush ended in an ominous silence. This was it. He could feel it in his bones.

Derek kept his gaze on the tree line and waited. A moment later he was rewarded with several camouflaged individuals breaking into the moonlight. He knew his men would wait on his signal, and he waited to see what the terrorists did before he gave the order to attack.

The first male, taller than the others, moved forward and knelt by the lake's edge. A second one handed him a cylinder of liquid, which they quickly attached to a long hose.

Derek whispered into his Sataphone. "Move out. Hostiles have arrived."

Chapter Nine

Dark shadows merged into the space behind the terrorists. Black garb, night goggles, and stealth should insure they were upon the terrorists before they were noticed.

The first objective would be to take out the man with the distribution device. No way could the chemicals be released into the lake. Derek moved forward and prayed his men would be successful in taking out the rearguard of the cell.

He shouldered his rifle and debated taking a shot. He didn't want to hit the cylinder. Better to get in close and use his Ka-Bar. The utility knife with its eleven and three-quarter inch blade would do the job without a loud hello.

Thankfully the moon chose that moment to hide behind a cloud. Derek quickened his pace as his magnified night vision spotlighted the first terrorist submerging the hose into the water.

Twenty feet from the hostile, Derek could hear the muffled whispers of the cell. He needed to move fast or he would miss his chance. They were a scant moment or two from discharging the chemicals.

He lunged his body into air and tackled the man holding the device, knocking him into the sand-and-stone lake edge. The device hit the ground before Derek could catch it in his hands, but a quick glance showed the chemicals were still in place.

The terrorist elbowed Derek in the gut, and then punched and jabbed him in the face. He returned the favor, trying to get the upper hand. Instead he found a knife similar to his own glinting in the reemerging moonlight.

He dodged the jab and brought his Ka-Bar to bear against the man's chest. The man twisted and tried to get away, and when he couldn't, he slammed his blade into Derek's stomach.

Pain lanced his insides like hot metal. He tried to ignore the sensation as he brought his knife back to its target. A quick flick and the man's curse died on his lips. A second later the man followed as a blood filled rattle issued from his throat.

Derek cursed as he felt the blood soaking his pants, and climbed to his knees. The device lay where it fell, and he yanked it back from the lake's edge. His men were still containing the other terrorists. He berated the weakness encasing his limbs, and fought the darkness threatening to take his vision. A swirl of color materialized near him right before he blacked out.

****

Catriona gazed in horror at the blood staining Derek's clothes. Her instinct was right. Even though he hadn't called her name out loud or whispered it in his mind, she'd known he was in trouble.

As she surveyed the chaos around her, she also knew that help would arrive too late for Derek if she didn't act. The others were still involved in hand-to-hand fighting. She could stop all of it by a wave of her hand, but did she dare?

To interfere with a mortal's destiny was something the court frowned upon. Maybe she could just freeze time until she could get Derek some help. And the only help that might save him lay in the faery realm. She'd never tried to heal another person, and too much magick could make his situation worse. He needed someone who knew what they were doing.

Catriona couldn't lose him, not now, and not like

this. She bent, placed her hand on his shoulder, and then zapped them both to her room in the palace.

She used magick to strip Derek of his clothes after she placed him on the bed. The wound was bleeding horribly. She needed help.

Their healer!

Before Catriona could flash out to seek Isabella's help, her da flashed in. His eyes glowed blue fire, his mouth opened, closed, and then opened again.

"Catriona! You have gone beyond any fae to date in bringing this mortal to our court." Her da's eyes flashed more fire and colors twirled from his fingertips: signs he was more than a bit irate.

"Da, I am sorry, but he's hurt badly, and he needs our help." Catriona didn't care if her statement was a plea. She would beg, cry, or get on her knees if it would help Derek.

"What is this man to you, daughter?" His voice was harsh, and Catriona knew he now acted in the form of king, although he used the word *daughter*.

"A friend, a man who tried to stop an enemy from polluting his country's water supply. He is a soldier who is in need of our help. I beg you to allow the healer to take care of him."

"I ask you again, what is this man to you?" Her da's voice dropped an octave in timbre, but he still pinned her with his gaze.

"He is the man I choose as my mate. The only man I will ever have if he will have me." Catriona spilled the words out and then waited to see what her da would do. Derek still lay immobile, and she feared she may have signed his death warrant and possibly her own. The court which was made up of other aristocracy from various realms could be brutal when their laws were disobeyed.

"To take a mortal as a mate goes against all of our rules. Are you sure, Catriona? The repercussions could be serious." Her da's voice was husky with emotion, and she thought she saw a glimmer of tears in his gaze.

"Yes. I love him. I don't want to be mated to someone who won't love me for me. He sees past the princess and to the woman inside of me, Da. Please save him!" Catriona felt the moisture on her face, and realized she was crying. Something she rarely did.

"Very well, I will summon Isabella. However you do realize that you could be severely punished. The others on the court could banish you from the fae world for a time or forever. Or they could take your magick."

A chill teased Catriona spine. She didn't want to give up her home. And giving up her magick would leave a huge hole in her chest, but nothing compared to losing Derek.

"I know, Da, but if he dies, I won't care about anything but dying anyway."

"Daughter, I love you, and will do all I can to make it right with the court." Her da caressed her cheek, and then called for the healer.

The next moments seemed to drag by, even though the healer arrived almost the instant her da called. Catriona welcomed her da's arm around her shoulders as they watched Isabella touch the wound and then sprinkle different herbs onto Derek's stomach.

Several long sighs later, Catriona jerked to attention when the healer turned their way. "King Tiernan, I have done all I can. His wound is grievous, but the bleeding has stopped. He will need to be watched for fever." Isabella waved her hands in the air. "I am sorry, I could not do more. He is mortal and I've never tried to heal one of their kind before now."

Tiernan nodded when Isabella curtsied to both him and Catriona. "Thank you. I will make sure you are rewarded for your efforts."

"My reward will be if the man lives." Isabella shook her dark hair back from her shoulders, and her blue-eyed gaze darted to Catriona. "If I'm not mistaken, this man is meant for great things, and is important to the princess."

"You are correct. Again my thanks."

"And mine, Isabella." Catriona smiled at the healer as she slid from beneath her da's arm. She moved to Derek's side. His bronze tone had paled, his lids slightly blue, and his lips were bled of color. She knew Isabella had indeed done all she knew to help him. Catriona just hoped it was enough.

****

Derek woke to a dull ache in his gut. He tried to remember what he'd eaten to cause the problem, and then it hit him. The mission! He raised his head, and then blinked his eyes at the sight in front of him.

Catriona lay sprawled across the foot of the bed, and a man not much older than him in looks sat in an ornate chair near Cat. Who was the man, and where was he?

"Cat?" His query sounded like a cross between a bull moose and a weak kitten.

"Derek!" Catriona almost somersaulted off the bed, and the man jerked awake. The crown on his head almost toppled off as he straightened up and leaned forward. In the same moment, Cat scrambled up to sit beside Derek.

Her hands touched and gently explored his gut. A gut that felt better by the minute. Then she put a hand to his forehead, held it there, before kissing him on the lips. "You're all right. No fever."

Then Catriona burst into tears.

"Ah, Cat, don't cry." Derek caressed her hair as she sobbed all over his chest.

"Daughter, the mortal is fine. Enough." The man, who if he wasn't losing his mind, must be Cat's father, stood up and moved to Derek's side of the bed.

"I am Tiernan, King of the Tuatha de Danann. My daughter has told me you are a good man. I prefer to make my own assessment."

Derek refused to even blink at the king's frown. He was sure the man thought himself to be intimidating, but after over a decade of being chewed out by the best the Marine Corps had to offer when he didn't always follow orders, Derek was immune to intimidation.

"Fair enough. I wouldn't have it any other way." He gently caught Cat's chin in his hand and raised her head to look at him. "Come on, darling. I'm fine. Not sure how that happened but I'm okay. Can I assume I'm not in my world anymore?"

Catriona giggled and then her face grew serious. "No, I had to bring you home with me. I didn't know how to fix you. Your men were busy and you were bleeding badly."

His men!

"What about my men? Are they okay?" Derek slid to the edge of the bed forcing the king to move back a pace.

"Derek, wait, they were fine when we left. They will be fine until you go back to them." Catriona shot a sideways glance at the king.

"Catriona, what did you do?" Her dad's growl made Cat flinch. Derek didn't like that one bit.

"Hey, don't growl at her." His legs were a bit wobbly as he gained his feet, but his shoulders were straight as he stood nose to nose with the king.

"And what will you do to stop me, mortal?"

"Well, if you want to fight man-to-man and leave off the girly crown and the domineering attitude, then I'll be happy to show you." Derek dared the king to take him up on his offer.

What he got was a genuine smile.

"Well done. If you are going to be my daughter's mate, then you must be able to hold your own with me or any other fae."

Derek took the hand he offered, shook it, and then turned to Catriona. "Now, tell me exactly what you did, please."

"I didn't do that much, truly." Catriona eased off her side of the bed. He wondered if she thought what she had to tell them would be better said with the bed length between them.

"And that would be?" Derek kept his tone calm, but he wondered how long it would last.

"I merely stopped time." Catriona waved her hand, and her body began to shimmer.

"Stop. You can't just leave every time something is not to your liking." Derek ignored her tear-drenched eyes, but he was relieved she didn't continue to zap her body away.

"I didn't mean to upset you or you." She turned to her da. "I just wanted to get Derek away."

Derek couldn't fault her for that; he'd be dead if she hadn't brought him here.

"What's done is done. You will go back with Derek and restart time. Let him finish his job and then I want you both back here to be wed. Is that clear?" The king looked at Cat.

"Yes, if Derek's agreeable." The look she gave him would have melted his heart if she hadn't already stolen it.

"It is, but there are a few things we need to straighten out." He hoped they could work out the logistics of their totally different lifestyles.

"I assume you have not soiled my daughter?" The king's question brought a rush of heat to Derek's face. He might not have taken Cat's virginity, but he'd come close.

"No, she is still innocent." He glanced at Cat who in turn looked at the floor.

"Good, then I will not have you castrated before your wedding night." The king sounded serious, and Derek resisted the urge to flinch.

"Glad to hear it, Pops. Now, Cat, let's go."

Derek's chuckle at the king's growl coincided with the world shimmering around him. The next moment he lay several feet from the terrorists. He looked at his men. All were alive and accounted for, thank God.

He called for Homeland Security to pick up their prisoners, and greeted his men before calling his commander. When he hung up he apprised them. "Commander says we get two extra weeks of R&R. So pack up and have fun. See you on base in a month."

Chapter Ten

Catriona watched as their wedding guests danced in time to the music. Raven and Wulf seemed to be having a good time also, and for once her sister and niece were behaving. Of course she'd threatened them both if they said one word to her matron of honor and Wulf. She'd also warned them to keep their distance from her new husband.

She smiled as her gaze found Derek's across the room where he stood talking with her da. The men seemed to be getting along wonderfully. It made her a bit apprehensive, but also happy. She wanted the most important men in her life to get along.

Derek's grin was just one of the things she loved about him. His charm, when he wasn't frowning at her for using magick, his determined gaze when it came to instructing her what to expect as a Marine wife, and the delicious way he held her when she just needed a hug.

And although they had not yet completely made love, he'd given her pleasure unlimited. It had only been a week since his successful mission and his healed injury, but it had passed extremely fast.

Her da had insisted on a full fae wedding. He'd balked at first about having Raven and Wulf in attendance but then he'd caved in, as Raven would say. Now, he actually seemed to have warmed up to the idea of non-faes in the palace. Which was wonderful. She'd love to introduce Raven to some of the pleasures she enjoyed while at home.

"Hey, babe." Derek's soft greeting sent a shiver

of delight down her spine. She hadn't realized he or her da had moved.

"Hello. I see you two are getting to know one another." She arched a brow at both men.

"Yes, daughter, my new son-in-law has been regaling me with some of his operations. I admit he might turn out to be a good match for you." Her da winked at Catriona before smirking at Derek. Oh well, at least they were behaving for now. And she gave her husband high marks for pointedly looking away. She wondered what he was thinking.

"Have you decided where you are going to live?" The king's question pinged into Derek's thoughts. Everything here in the Seelie Court had a surreal quality to it. The entire palace, which he had not seen until the wedding, was decked out in flowers, garlands of greenery, and food galore. Thank God his new father-in-law liked his meat as much as Derek did. He'd been afraid he'd have to make do with minute portions of fruit, finger sandwiches, and ambrosia. Although the beverage did have quite a kick.

"Yes, when I'm not on an op, Cat will be living with me. When I'm in the field, she is going to come to you. This way I know she's safe and..."

"Stays out of trouble." The king finished his unspoken thought.

"Hey, I am not a child. Don't treat me as one. I plan to be the perfect wife." Catriona's lips were turned up in a bit of a pout that he would dearly love to kiss away. He glanced at his watch but it seemed that once in the fae world time stopped.

"And I know you will be." Derek took advantage of the invitation her open mouth elicited and kissed her lightly on the lips. He then whispered in her ear. "How much longer do we need to stay at this shindig?"

Catriona's cheeks bloomed with color as she met

his gaze. "As far as I'm concerned we can leave now." She caught her da's arm and pulled his attention back to them and away from the dancing.

"Da, Derek and I are leaving."

"But we have not toasted your nuptials yet." The king did not look overly pleased.

"I don't suppose you could do it without us?" She shot Derek a look that caused his sex to harden like day-old cement.

"No, but I promise to make it quick." The king tried to smile at Cat, but he looked miserable. Derek couldn't blame him; he'd feel the same way about his own daughter.

"King Tiernan, I will do nothing to dishonor Catriona. I love her." He held his hand out and her dad shook hands with him.

"I know. It is not easy being a da to my daughters without their mother being here." The King's gaze seemed blank for a moment as if he were remembering the woman who bore Catriona. A second later, he shrugged his massive shoulders and gave a slight smile.

"I know things have been chaotic but you have not said anything about possible reprisals for what Cat did," Derek commented, and when the king raised a brow, he responded.

"Cat told me what you said. Will she be punished?" Derek hoped not, but come what may, she would be protected by him and the entire Marine Corps if necessary.

"No, I spoke with the court, and after extensive debates, Catriona will not suffer for her deeds." Tiernan looked off in the distance for a moment. Derek wondered what was up with that look, but decided after all the king had done for them, he'd allow the man his own counsel.

The king turned back to face Derek and Catriona. "Come, let's toast your wedding. Friends, family, may I have your attention please."

Tiernan's booming baritone stilled the music, the chattering, and even the servers as they took care of the guests' needs. He took two goblets of ambrosia from a server, handed one to Derek, and the other to Catriona, before taking one for himself and raising it high.

"Tonight we celebrate the marriage of my oldest daughter, Catriona, who will one day rule in my stead. Her new husband has proven himself to be honest, brave, and more than worthy to rule at her side when that time comes. Now raise your glasses and drink to their health, prosperity, happiness, and"—he looked at Derek and laughed—"and an abundance of daughters."

Derek choked as he took a swallow of fruity liquid. Catriona patted him gently on the back, whereas his father-in-law pounded the daylights out of him. Once he got his breath back, he spat, "Enough, your majestic pain in the—"

"Derek!" Catriona's shocked cry coincided with the king's hearty boom of laughter. Before he could apologize Catriona waved her hand and they were gone.

The week before their wedding he'd spent some time at his base, filing reports, etc, but had called Catriona at Raven's. She'd begged him to let her choose the place they would honeymoon. He'd agreed. But now looking at the dark clouds overhead and the menacing forest they stood in front of, he wondered if he should have called a travel agency.

"Come on, you'll love it here. It's my favorite place to hide from others. Only I and now you know of its existence."

"Hon, are you sure you know what you're doing?" Derek didn't want to upset his bride, but where on Earth did she think they were going to consummate their marriage?"

"Of course, silly. This is a mirage to keep others out. It will be fine. Trust me." Cat caught his hand and tugged him into the dense trees. The moment they were about ten feet into the stand of oaks, the entire scene changed. Moonlight flooded a beautiful valley and highlighted the ripples on a nearby lake.

"How on Earth..." He didn't finish his sentence because Cat grabbed his arm and started tugging him forward once again. "Derek, you will love this place. It's so peaceful, and I believe that is something you've not had enough of in your life." Her expression was serious, her gaze expectant and a bit apprehensive.

Derek stopped his beautiful wife's forward momentum and turned her toward him. His lips captured hers. He didn't know how he could ever tell her what it meant to him that she loved him and had ferreted out the one thing he'd always kept hidden.

Once he ended their kiss, much to Catriona's apparent disappointment, not to mention how hard his rod ached, he lifted her in his arms.

"I love you, you know that, don't you?" He hoped so with all his heart.

"Of course I do. Just like I love you. Now, come see the house. I think you will love the view."

"The only view I want to see is you, woman, naked." Derek growled the words and laughed when Cat did.

A second later, a cabin as big as the barracks he'd been bunking before getting his apartment ready for a bride, came into view. A deck wrapped around the structure, giving it a rustic and homey feel.

He hurried his pace and climbed the few steps to the porch. After opening the door, he carried Cat over the threshold. The room blazed with a fire in the giant hearth, food lay on the counter dividing the living area from the kitchen, and candles lit the stairway going up to the second floor.

Derek detoured to the counter, grabbed a bottle of champagne, two glasses, and placed them gently in Cat's arms. Now he was ready to make his bride a wife, completely.

The steps were just a slight impediment in his rush to get to the main bedroom, and having the door open magically was something he could get used to in time.

He set Cat on her feet, took the glasses and bottle from her, and placed them on a table near the bed. Then he backed her to the bed and followed her body downward. His mouth found hers and he tasted the sweet ambrosia she'd had earlier. Derek's hands sought the bottom of her iridescent, multi-colored gown and pulled it up her legs, thighs, waist, and then over her head.

"Derek, no fair, I want to undress you too." Cat's sultry tone caused his sex to rise up and tent the front of his dress blue pants.

He gazed at the sight before him. Cat's silver blonde hair curled and took control of the pillow she lay on. Her blue eyes shone as bright as the flame of a candle. Her lips were slightly swollen and were turned up in a come-to-me smile.

Never in all his life and travels had he ever seen such radiant beauty. Her breasts were encased in an almost cobweb like lace, so fine, he was fearful he would tear it with his hands as he tried to find a way to get to her trapped beauty.

Her center was as elusive as the rest of her curves. Dammit, he was a Marine. He should be able to figure out how to get her stripped without making a mess of her whatever it was.

"Derek, if you don't hurry, I'm going to make my own move." Cat gave him a look he couldn't misunderstand.

"I'm trying, but I don't see any buttons or snaps

on this thing." His voice shook with an over abundance of lust.

Her laughter caressed his heart, but he wanted to caress her body.

"Allow me." Catriona didn't so much as raise her hand but the next second she was naked.

"Think you can teach me to do that?" Derek asked as he nibbled on the slim column of Cat's throat. His lips soon followed a path to her breasts. Decisions, decisions, which one to suckle first?

Catriona gasped as Derek's tongue did a slow slide up the underside of her breast and then swirled around her nipple. The tip elongated and she shivered with expectancy. She wasn't disappointed. Derek caught the tip between his teeth and lightly nipped. Her hips began to move on the bed. Her senses were alive with desire for this man. She wanted him so much it hurt to breathe.

"Derek." Her moan erupted at the same time he caressed the other breast. She gripped his shoulders.

"Steady, love, I'm just getting warmed up." Derek's words even more so than his sexy rumble caused her core to weep with want.

"If I get any warmer, I'll burst into flames..."

"Well, that's what I want you to do." Derek plundered her body as if it were one of his missions, or so Catriona thought. He moved ahead like he was on reconnaissance. His lips kissed and licked her stomach before moving toward the object of her ache. But instead of giving her what she wanted, Derek bypassed her sex and began to kiss the inside of her thighs.

The man knew how to torture. Catriona opened her legs and allowed him better access. She held her breath as he moved down her legs, kissed the inside of her arches, and moved upward once more. She let her breath out in a rush when he kissed the underside of her knees, drawing first one leg and then the other over his shoulders. She gripped the sheets with her hands when his tongue touched her molten center. Her hips left the mattress to push even closer to his weapon of choice. The snake of desire took hold, and Catriona felt the first ripple of her climax strike. Its grip was so strong she lost her breath. She moved her hands to his head and held him as her body began to spasm and continued to do so until every bone she had was fluid, every muscle a weak imitation, and the pleasure so intense she almost passed out.

Derek's body trembled with a lust that he almost couldn't control. If he didn't get a handle on it, he would be jumping the gun—something that had not happened to him since he was a teenager.

He slowed his breathing and watched as Cat's body stopped trembling, and then she opened her eyes. Her blue gaze still looked a bit blank, but the beginning of a smile creased her lips. He got to his knees and leaned forward to kiss each corner of her smile before delving inside. Kissing for him had always been a prelude to making love, something women expected. With Cat he wanted to taste her sweetness, to hear her moan while he plundered and danced with her tongue.

But enough was enough; he wanted her as a man wanted a woman. This time he prayed she wouldn't disappear. A man could only stand so much.

He pulled her hips forward and up. He tried to smile at Cat, but every muscle in his body seemed to be centered between his legs. Derek pushed forward, and Catriona didn't flinch—good. Of course he was a long way from breaching her virginity. He inched forward a bit more. Then a few more inches. His wife's eyes were now open wide, a pulse beat danced in her throat. Was it from wanting him or fear? Maybe both?

This time when he moved he flexed his hand over her mons and stroked the tiny offering hidden so delicately with his forefinger. Catriona began to move her hips, just a bit, but that was good. She was back in the game, and he wanted to make sure she stayed that way.

When her body began to tremble, he waited one moment and then thrust to the max. Her body went stiff when he dispensed with her cherry and then she closed her eyes. He pulled almost all the way out and then thrust forward once again.

"Derek, I don't think I can go up in flames again." Catriona moaned her words. They were music to his ears.

"You can and will. Only this time, I'll be with you."

Again he pulled out and then pushed back in. A moment later, Cat's hips rose to meet his every movement. He welcomed the feel of her body clamped around him. He could feel the liquid desire easing his way, making him go deeper. His sac tightened, his length grew, and he felt the first rasp of his orgasm. He moved faster, rotating his hips against Cat, until he thought the sensation would burst him at the seams.

Derek braced his body, felt the hot rush of completion, and then a roar left his throat. Cat fell at the same time, her scream an accompaniment to their shared climax.

****

Catriona snuggled next to Derek's heart and felt the weightlessness of being loved over and over again. She and her husband had made delicious love while she was on her knees, sitting on his lap, and lying on her side.

Never in her wildest imagination and her years of being fae would she have dreamed being loved by this man to be the most perfect feeling in both their worlds.

Derek stirred just a bit and pulled her even closer. She welcomed the feel of his naked body next to hers, and reveled in the fact his man-root was even now stirring once more.

"Babe, you're killing me," he rumbled.

"I'm doing nothing, my husband, but trying to catch my breath." Catriona laughed.

"Then could you do it without moving? I don't think I have the stamina to make love for at least another hour." Derek grinned down at her.

"Well, why don't you open the champagne? I'm thirsty." Catriona licked her lips in anticipation of a cold drink.

"Hey, you're the one with magick in her fingertips. You do it." Derek nuzzled her neck.

"Fine, but don't get used to me waiting on you. Raven told me how men can be." Catriona teased him.

"Well, look at what Rav married. He's kind of a throwback. Oh wait, he is that old."

"Be nice. I'm really glad my da allowed them to celebrate with us." Catriona waved her hand and then handed Derek a glass of champagne before sipping from hers.

"Yeah, tell you the truth so am I. And I'm really glad you love me." Derek's voice went all wobbly for a moment and then his tone was strong once again when he whispered. "I love you, Catriona, Princess of the Tuatha de Danann."

"I love you too, and I think my da is warming up to you nicely."

When Derek growled she giggled again.

"What's so funny?" he asked.

"I was thinking about his toast before we left."

"Yeah, what was up with that? An abundance of daughters?" Derek took a sip before continuing. "Don't get me wrong, I would love a little girl like you but I want boys too."

"Well, I hope you won't be disappointed if we have a girl the first time." Catriona waited to see what Derek would say before she dropped the equivalent of a ton on his dream.

"How can you be sure it won't be a son?" He sounded confused more than anything.

"Uh, if I'm not mistaken, the ambrosia we drank for our toast was mixed with a fertility spell."

Derek set up so fast, droplets of champagne sprinkled Cat's body.

"A fertility spell? What the hell is that?" His growl made her want to laugh. Derek looked so adorable, so irate, so confused, and so scared she decided not to.

"It's a spell that insures a couple will be blessed with many children." Catriona purposely kept her tone calm.

"And I suppose all those children will be girls" Derek raked a hand through his hair. She couldn't help but notice it trembled slightly.

"You could say that." When Derek growled again, she hastily inserted. "But then again, there should be boys also."

The Derek she knew and loved seemed to get a grip on his emotions. He wiped a drop of liquid off her cheek, looked her full in the face, and then opened his mouth.

"Is there anything else I need to know about our proposed offspring?" His green gaze stayed constant, his pupils didn't react to what she knew had to be a shock.

"I uh, I..." Catriona wasn't sure she could tell him and keep a straight face.

"Cat, what is it?"

"Well, according to some of our legends, and mind you they are legends, if a fae marries a mortal, which is very rare and as you know forbidden, then all of the daughters will be fae."

Derek's mouth opened but no words came out.

"Are you okay? Derek?" Catriona shook him. His silence and stillness frightened her.

"Please say something, anything," she pleaded.

"Semper Fi and magick, who would have thought." He pulled her close, kissed her lips, and then one word echoed through the room. "Oooohrah."

****

Tiernan took a sip of ambrosia and immediately set the glass down. It tasted like ashes. He gazed out over the back gardens of the castle. The landscape still held the remnants of his daughter's wedding. A bond that would cost him dearly. What he had not divulged to her new husband was the only reason the members of the court did not punish Catriona was he bartered himself in her place.

Now he waited for his sentence to be pronounced and carried out. A shimmer of color twisted across the horizon. The time had come. Soon he would know his punishment.

About the author...

Faith started her journey to publication when she joined the Romance board at iVillage.com, where she became a community leader. She has written book reviews for *Bridges* magazine, MyShelf.com and Romantic Times Book Reviews. She also pens a column for a local magazine.

Her path veered into editing and marketing for a small press before she joined The Wild Rose Press staff. Her dream of having her own work published is a blessing and an honor.

Faith resides in the South with her daughter Amanda, memories of her now-angel husband Rick, and a special zoo crew of furry babies.

Visit her at www.faithvsmith.com

Other books by Faith V. Smith:
Beware What You Wish
Kensington's Soul
Dunbar's Curse
Viking, Go Home
Gideon's Heart

Coming soon from The Wild Rose Press:

IMMORTAL JUSTICE
Book 1 of The Immortal Executioners

To My Readers...

What can I say but to tell you how much you all mean to me! Writing is a passion, but one that is so much more enjoyable knowing someone besides myself and my editor love my work.

I hope you enjoyed Derek and Catriona's story. Please look forward to a third book featuring Tiernan, Catriona's da, who is way too hot not to have his own romance. King of the Seelie Court, he can also be the king of hearts.

~**Faith V. Smith**

www.ingramcontent.com/pod-product-compliance
Lightning Source LLC
Chambersburg PA
CBHW072141170626
46813CB00004BA/1637